HILLBILLY CHOIR

HILLBILLY CHOIR

Rhea Beth Ross

Houghton Mifflin Company
Boston   1991

Also by Rhea Beth Ross
The Bet's On, Lizzie Bingman!

c. 1

Library of Congress Cataloging-in-Publication Data
Ross, Rhea Beth.
  Hillbilly choir / Rhea Beth Ross.
    p. cm.
  Summary: Returning in 1932 to the rural community in Arkansas
where she grew up, fifteen-year-old Laurie is torn between staying
in the comfortable place she loves and allowing her ambitious mother
to aid her burgeoning singing career.
  ISBN 0-395-53356-2
  [1. Family life — Fiction.   2. Arkansas — Fiction.   3. Singers —
Fiction.]   I. Title.
PZ7.R71983Hi   1991   90-40825
[Fic] — dc20   CIP
                            AC

Printed in the United States of America

AGM 10 9 8 7 6 5 4 3 2 1

To Donald and Autumn and Nathan

HILLBILLY CHOIR

1

There was only one road leading to Guthrie, Arkansas. It was a narrow path covered with pebbles, stones, and, after a hard rain, boulders.

It must have rained for several days before Mama and I crossed the state line because those boulders were popping up and threatening the tires of Mama's brand-new Packard. The automobile was a deluxe model complete with a V-12 engine, wire wheels, and all the other luxuries salesmen said were very important on the 1932 models.

We hit a rock and heard a loud pop. Mama slammed on the brakes and the auto slid, nose first, into a ditch. She cut the engine and wiped her forehead with the back of her hand.

"I should have known better than to drive out here," Mama said.

"Blown tire?" I asked.

She opened the door. "Blown tire."

"Do we have a patch?"

"We do, but I don't know how to put it on." Mama got out, checked the tire, and stared down the road. "We'll sit tight for a while. Maybe someone will come along."

On a weekday, sitting and waiting for someone to "come along" outside Guthrie would have been a stupid thing to do, but it was Friday and most families traveled to Crossroads to the general store to buy supplies for the next week.

1

Mama dusted off the hood of the Packard and scooted up on it, letting her legs dangle over the side as if she were a child. She patted a place beside her, so I got out of the automobile and climbed onto the shiny yellow seat.

"I needed some time to talk with you," Mama said. "This gives us a few moments to ourselves before we get to the farm."

"Thought we'd said it all," I mumbled, remembering how hard the last few weeks had been since Mama had lost her job at the Arcadia Theatre in New York. It hadn't been her fault. She had been good on stage, but all her friends were headed to Hollywood to break into talkies, so they shut down the play they had been in. Mama was left, in her own words, "high and dry." She could have gone with them to California, but she said that was too far from home.

Until we actually reached Arkansas I was afraid Mama would change her mind and drive us to the coast. I had seen picture postcards from Mama's friends. Everyone there seemed to be going to parties in the sunshine. Mama did like parties.

"I couldn't make it in New York," Mama said with a sweet, sad voice.

"It wasn't your fault."

She looked hard at me. "I tried."

"You made enough money to buy this automobile."

"Well . . . I want more. At least more for you. Guthrie has nothing to offer a young person. No job. No future. No hope."

"There are picnics and singings and Sunday suppers."

"Those suppers aren't free, and we don't have fifty dollars left."

"Nannie will take us in."

2

"I'm crawling back, like always. Every time I get ahead something goes wrong, and I end up back here in Guthrie."

"It's home," I said.

"I don't need to hear that. It will be the same old thing —"

"You're the one who wanted to talk," I reminded her.

"And you're a child, hardly able to preach to me."

"I'm fifteen! And I wasn't preaching."

Mama smiled as an apology.

"We did all right in New York," I said.

"We did okay, I guess, but I know you were lonely." Mama took hold of my hands and looked into my eyes.

I had been lonely. I had spent day after day in our apartment with only the radio and my guitar for company. Then there was that extra loneliness of watching Mama leave nearly every evening in one of her two "special" dresses. The red one for a "hot" producer she just had to meet. The black one she wore with a long white strand of fake pearls for the "rich" producer she just had to impress.

"You've forgotten how much fun it is at Nannie's," I said with an enthusiasm I hoped would infect her. "She'll pamper us and feed us peaches and cream."

"I know."

"And there's Star. We haven't seen her in over two years. Think of all the fun we'll have this summer catching up on things."

Mama smiled. "It'll be great," she said with a hollow voice.

"It will be great," I said, wishing I could tell her how happy I was to be back in Arkansas. But I knew that that would hurt her feelings.

"I don't think anyone is coming. Maybe we'd better walk to Crossroads Store and get some help," Mama said. She went over to look in the side-view mirror and fluffed her hair.

Mama was mostly blond on her own, but she had been applying peroxide to the sides of her hair to make it even more flaxen. She straightened up. "I'd put on a little lipstick, but Aunt Nola may be at the house and I don't think I can stand to hear her pray to Jesus about my sinful 'paint.'"

Mama chose to walk through the meadow instead of along the road. She said it was to avoid the mud, but I suspected it was because she liked the feel of the soft grass under her bare feet, as I did. I walked behind her and decided that the way she looked right then, with her stockings thrown over her shoulders and her high heels pinched like captive butterflies in her hands, would be the way I would always remember her.

Ada Thomas met us on the front porch of the store. "Well, I'll declare, look who's come traipsing across the field. Come out, Mel. See the company," she called through the screen door.

Mel Thomas, wiping his hands on his butcher's apron, joined his wife on the porch. "This calls for some sodie pop," he said, smiling at Mama before he hurried over to the cooler beside the door.

"Did Nan know you were coming today?" Ada asked as she nudged Mama toward a chair.

"She's expecting us," Mama answered as she slipped on her shoes.

Mel was back by then, holding two tall bottles of grape Nehi toward Mama and me. "What are you doing on foot, without your bags?" he asked as he surveyed the road.

"My auto blew a tire," Mama said after she had taken a long drink of the soda. "We were hoping to find someone to help us."

Ada said, "Been busy all day, slacked off now. Expect near everyone in the county has been in. 'Course there's always a few folks runnin' late with their chores."

4

Mel sat down on a little stool and scooted toward Mama. "Heard you made it big in the theater business. Heard you're driving an automobile that's as slick as a weasel and shinier than a prize hog."

"I've had a couple of parts," Mama said softly.

"Seen any really big-time stars?" Mel persisted.

Mama sighed.

"She met Mary Pickford," I said with a big smile. Mama was being so unfriendly.

"Lordy, lordy," Ada squealed. "Mary Pickford. You met her? Up close and all that? Is she as sweet in person as she is on the screen? I saw her in a moving picture over at —"

Mama interrupted, "Miss Pickford's an actress. She can be sweet at the drop of a hat."

"Suppose we should get *your* audygraph before you make a name for yourself," Mel said.

"Save your ink," Mama said sullenly.

Ada and Mel didn't speak.

Mama finally smiled. "I'm sorry. I didn't mean for that to sound the way it did." Then Mama stood up and walked across the porch. "Mel, it doesn't look like a parade is going to pass by. Could I get you to send someone you trust out to patch the tire on my automobile and drive it over to Nan's?" Mama said.

Mel stood up and slapped his knee. "I'll go myself if it means getting a turn behind the wheel of a machine like you're supposed to have."

Mama took hold of my hand and led me off the porch.

Ada called after us, "'Spect I'll be seeing more of ya."

Mama waved over her shoulder, then mumbled, "Why me?"

"What do you mean?" I asked.

Mama squeezed my hand. "Why am I stuck here right

now? California, why it might as well be as far away as the moon. All my friends are going to be there. And I'm going to be in Guthrie, rooted like one of the big sycamores by the river."

The Wigerstat River was still running alongside the road; the land was still the same pea green color; and the birds were still singing their sweet, high courting calls from the stand of pines near the water. It was as if Mama and I had never been away.

As I thought she would, Mama began to hum. It was an old tune, one about a love that had gone wrong. The notes rose above the pines and mingled with the bird songs.

Mama slid her arm around my waist and pulled me close. "Sing for me, Laurie. Sing that sweet song about coming home."

I sang. At first it came out as a warble until I got the rhythm timed with our fast walking. Then it turned into a hymn and then something of an anthem. Mama joined in, and we sang at the top of our lungs. Our voices carried to the hilltops, free from the drone of the city.

Suddenly, Mama stopped walking and hugged me hard. "It'll be all right, Laurie. There's no shame in going home to rest for a while. Everyone needs a little rest, a little time to sort things out."

I said, "Yes, Mama," but she was comforting only herself. I had no doubts; I wanted to be home.

Nannie's place hadn't changed any since we had been gone, unless you counted a different scarecrow at the edge of her acre garden.

The scarecrow was dressed in a patched suit that looked like the one Mr. Avartoz used to wear on his yearly trip to the synagogue in Kansas City. Mr. Avartoz and several other nearly indescribable characters boarded with Nannie. They lived in their respective rooms on the top floor of Nannie's three-story farmhouse. Rooming with them was like having a half dozen grandparents, but Nannie was the only one I had to listen to.

As Mama and I walked up the driveway, the big screen porch buzzed. Mrs. Appleton, who everyone called "Apples," bounded out of her rocking chair and hurried into the house. The Baker twins, Ezra and Nehemiah, stood up slowly, leaning on each other for support. Old Mrs. Turner laid her knitting aside and waved at us.

"The gang's all here," I said, waving back.

"They smell like liniment and prunes," Mama said disgustedly.

"We'll get used to it." I smiled at Mama as she hurried up the front walk.

I knew Mama doubted it, especially when the Baker twins tackled her with a hug when she walked onto the porch.

Nannie came out then. She wore her white baker's apron and was covered with flour from her hands to her elbows. When Nannie held out her arms, Mama ran to her. They held each other for a long time. Finally, Mama stood back and wiped away her tears.

Nannie looked at the others, who were weeping in various volumes. "This isn't a funeral. It's a homecoming," Nannie reminded them as she pulled me to her and gave me a bone-crushing hug. "I've missed you, granddaughter. I've worried about you."

"I missed you too," I whispered.

"I'm baking," Nannie said.

"So I see," I answered, tracing a path in the flour on her arm. "I hope it's strawberry shortcake."

"Fresh-picked berries," Nannie said, smiling.

7

I glanced toward the yard.

Nannie said, "If you're looking for Star, she rode into Harrisburg with Mr. Avartoz. We didn't expect you to arrive until later this evening."

Star was Mama's little sister. A star in the dark night of old people. Star had never liked living among them. I knew there was nothing wrong with the boarders. They had wonderful stories to tell, and most of them could cook delicious treats. Some of their recipes came from "The Old Country" hidden in their hearts; others were concocted on the white-hot stove of hard times. But Star didn't seem to care to know anything about the boarders' pasts. To her they were intruders, and that was that.

Nannie led us into the kitchen and served us fried chicken left over from lunch and fresh lettuce wilted with hot bacon grease. She wouldn't let me eat the shortcake because it was for supper; but I did have berries and thick, sweet cream.

While we ate, the boarders kept appearing at the kitchen door to peek at us. Every time Nannie looked away, Mama would glare at the spies and make a shooing motion with her hand.

"They're curious," Nannie said when she finally caught Mama waving violently at Mrs. Turner.

"We haven't seen each other in two years. You would think they would have the common courtesy to give us a few minutes alone," Mama spat.

Nannie didn't answer Mama but instead walked over to the door and talked to the boarders. They began to drift by the kitchen door on the way to their chairs on the porch.

Nannie came back and poured us iced tea. "Nice to have you girls home," she said softly as she sat down.

"Nice to be back," I said. I turned to Mama, wishing she would say the same thing, but, instead, she reached for her handbag and pulled out a short clipping taken from the *New York Times*.

"About you?" Nannie asked as she put on her spectacles. She took the paper and read aloud, "Miss Sierra Gabriella shows notable promise."

Mama shifted in her seat.

Nannie turned the clipping over. The back side was an advertisement for Carter's Little Pills.

"That's all there is, Nan," Mama said softly.

Nannie glanced at the clipping again and asked, "You're Sierra Gabriella?"

Mama ducked her head. "Sarah Hargrove didn't sound ritzy enough, so I changed Sarah to Sierra and used yours and Papa's name, Gabriel, with a little flourish."

"A little flourish," Nannie repeated. "Sarah to Sierra. Gabriel to Gabriella." She stood up. "That's show business."

Mama asked, "Are you angry?"

Nannie shook her head no.

"Are you disappointed?"

"Never in you."

"I love you, Nan."

Nannie walked toward the back porch. "And I love you, Sierra Gabriella."

When Nannie was out of the kitchen Mama looked long at me. "She wasn't impressed. I've always let her down."

"You don't have to impress Nannie," I said.

"No chance in doing that." Mama got up and cleared the table.

"What did you say in your letter to Nannie when you told her we were coming?"

"That we're broke. That I need a job. And that we would like to stay here for a while," Mama answered as she pumped water on the dishes.

"And what did Nannie say?"

Mama plunged her arms into the dishwater and began to scrub a pan. "She said there's always plenty of work here." Mama began to cry, softly at first and then with great, empty gasps.

I got up and went to her, putting my arms around her waist as she worked. "I'll finish the dishes. Why don't you go freshen up," I said.

Mama nodded and wiped her hands on a tea towel.

It was nearly suppertime when Mr. Avartoz eased his old Model T up to the barn. He got out quickly and shooed a flock of chickens away from the door so he could park his "beloved automobile out of the elements."

Star got out with a box in her hands and ran toward the house.

"Friends forever!" she cried, tossing the box beside the fence.

"Friends forever!" I yelled as I flew into her arms.

We whirled each other around until we were dizzy and fell onto the grass.

"What are you doing with those groceries?" Mr. Avartoz asked excitedly.

"Nothing," Star answered.

"You had better not have damaged those groceries, or Nan will be on you like a hawk on a rat," he said as he passed by us. "Laurie, you're nearly a woman. Where's your mama?"

I motioned inside, so Mr. Avartoz hurried up the back steps and slammed the door on the screen porch.

Star looked toward the grocery box. There was something running down its side. "We're together one minute, and you've already got me in trouble."

"I didn't throw the box," I said.

Star laughed and lay back on the grass. "Suppose you've noticed everything is the same as it was when you left?"

"Good old Guthrie," I said happily.

"But wait until you see how Nathan has grown." Star whistled low.

"You know, he didn't write me once," I told her.

"'Spect he was too busy."

"Two years of 'too busy'?"

"He's mighty fine looking. He's perfect for you. Perfect."

"If Nathan Graham is so fine, why aren't you trying to make him yours?" I teased.

Star huffed, "Not my type. Church boys are not my type. He's *your* type. He likes everything you like: lazy Sunday afternoons and big family dinners and . . . babies."

I smiled at Star. Even when she tried to sound annoyed, her words were tempered by her soft Southern drawl. Then, as if Star had read my mind, she said, "Know what, Laurie? You're talking kinda funny. Cuttin' off your words as if you're afraid to let them ease out of your mouth."

"New York, I guess."

"New York," she said dreamily. "I expect Sarah will tell me all about it."

"I was there, too," I reminded her.

Star smiled. "Your mama will tell it differently from you. Her letters were better than yours. She wrote about the theater. You wrote about the four walls in your apartment. Big difference."

"If you feel that way, then talk to her," I said.

Star sighed. "Wait until you see Cora."

I lay back. "How is Cousin Cora?"

"Ugly as ever. She would look better if someone reached down her throat, grabbed her by the toes, and pulled her inside out."

11

"That bad?"

"Worse. She has breasts now. And she pooches them out and moves them around," Star said, rolling side to side and sticking out her chest.

"Bet that drives Aunt Nola up the wall."

"She's been having special prayer meetings about it, I suspect," Star said, laughing. She stood up and pulled me to my feet. "Better carry these things into the house and let Nan yell at me over whatever's broken."

Star walked toward the box and peeked inside. "Good. It was the castor oil."

When Star set the box on the kitchen table, Nannie took one look at it and said, "Selective damage, I see."

Star braced herself for a lecture, but Nannie only began to put the groceries into the cupboard. Star looked at me with a face that asked, Is that it?

Nannie turned toward us. "Now, girls, you need to get ready to go to the singing before we have our supper."

Surprised, I said, "But Nannie, it's Friday night. The singings are on Saturday."

"Not anymore," Nannie said as she turned to look at Mama who had just walked into the kitchen.

"What's not anymore?" Mama asked as she hurried to Star and hugged her.

"The singings are held on Friday now. Thanks to radio," Nannie answered.

"Radio?" I asked.

"Folks don't want to miss their favorite programs," Nannie said. She walked toward the parlor, and we followed her.

There, beside the piano, sat a long, maple-colored radio.

"I don't believe it," Mama said as she walked over to touch it. "I can't believe you gave in and bought one."

"Didn't like the idea much," Nannie said, glancing at Star.

Mama said, "I also can't believe the singings are on Friday. They have been *the* thing to do on Saturdays for as many years as I can remember."

"It's getting more important to listen to someone play a few tunes than to make your own music," Nannie said hollowly as she and Star left the room.

Mama and I stood there for a moment.

"I guess things can change in Guthrie, Arkansas," Mama said happily.

"I guess they can," I agreed as I followed her into the hall. I glanced back into the parlor and noticed that the piano and the radio seemed to be staring each other down.

2

Eating at Nannie's table was like having a sweet dream. You drifted into the meal by sampling her relish tray of sweet pickles, chutney, piccalilli, and tiny stuffed mushrooms.

After the relish tray had been taken from the table, the serious eating began. Only then were we supposed to sit down and place our napkins in our laps. Nannie sat down at the head of the table after all the food was set before us. After that, she didn't get up to serve.

Apples was a jack-in-the-box, up to get this and up to get that. She guarded this function with a vengeance.

Mr. Avartoz sat at the opposite end of the table from Nannie. He had become the father of sorts of the ragtag group. He ate "like a bird," as Nannie would say, preferring to spend his mealtime talking.

Mama sat on the right side of Nannie. I sat next to her. Star sat by me in Mrs. Turner's regular place. I could tell Mrs. Turner was upset about the change in seating arrangements by the way she moped to her chair, but she didn't say anything. She merely settled down between the Baker twins and tried to avoid their jabbing elbows.

When Apples wasn't hopping up, she sat beside Mr. Avartoz. With only nine of us at the big oak harvest table, there should still have been plenty of room, but there wasn't. We sat fork to fork, and all because of one of Nannie's little quirks. There were two extra places set. Both were to Nan-

14

nie's immediate left. One place was set for Jesus, in case he should ever "drop in." The other was set for Nannie's only son, Eli, who went away to fight in the Great War and, like my daddy, didn't return.

There wasn't a place set for Daddy because he was buried in the little cemetery on the hill beside the Wigerstat Shoals Baptist Church. Uncle Eli didn't have a resting place. He was making his home in Little Rock. No one spoke of Eli around Nannie. He had betrayed her in no uncertain terms when he didn't come back from fighting and take over the farm. Neighbors saw him now and then and told us he had three little children. Nannie wouldn't listen to the gossip and vowed never to speak to Eli until he came home, begging forgiveness and asking, "What's for supper?"

"We'll pray now," Nannie said, folding her hands. She asked Jesus to bless the food.

Mr. Avartoz always sat open-eyed whenever Nannie prayed. When she had said "amen," he would bow his head and whisper some mumbo jumbo to Jehovah God. He didn't consider Nannie's end of the table kosher. It was their only difference.

I began to fill my plate and pass the bowls of food offered me as quickly as I could. When we all had full plates, Nannie said, "Let's begin."

First in my mouth was a big bite of mashed potatoes. It was such a big bite, Mama turned and glared at me. I couldn't help it. Nannie's mashed potatoes were the best in the world. They were rich and thick and made with warm cream and fresh butter, totally unlike the fake potatoes Mama and I had eaten at the diner next to our apartment.

Mama took a bite of potatoes, and an approving sound came from her lips, as if she couldn't stop it. "Sorry, Nan," she said softly.

15

Nannie smiled.

Mama turned to look at me, and I couldn't help but remember our first meal in New York City. It had been at a diner notorious for destroying taste buds. We'd had hot beef sandwiches. The beef was as tough as shoe leather, the bread was a week old, and the mashed potatoes were so thin they would have passed for soup if they'd been served in a bowl.

We called it our last meal. It was so awful I was surprised when Mama took a chance on dessert and paid twenty cents for two pieces of yellow pound cake wrapped individually in waxed paper.

We had taken the cake back to our apartment and had it with cups of weak tea. It wasn't half bad, but it wasn't home cooking. Mama cried then. It was the first time I had ever seen her weep openly. I figured she must have wanted to be a star very much to eat tanned beef and soupy potatoes. I vowed to myself never to complain.

"Missed your cooking, Nan," Mama said.

"They don't cook like this in New York City?" Nannie asked, beaming.

Mama looked miserable, so I said, "No one cooks like you."

Nannie smiled. "I believe that young lady wants extra shortcake."

Mama patted me on the leg, and I quickly caught her hand. We gave each other a squeeze and sealed that memory of pound cake and weak tea and weeping in the private world we had known.

Mama's Packard came flying up the driveway about six o'clock that evening. It wasn't Mel Thomas behind the wheel; it was Al Graham, Nathan's daddy, driving. Nathan was seated beside him. I could tell he was much taller than he had

16

been when Mama and I went to New York by the way he was peering out the passenger's window.

Nannie met them in the yard, calling, "Well, Reverend, don't you look as fancy as a feathered hat in that machine!"

Al Graham was the pastor of the Baptist church at Wigerstat Shoals, a small community on the far side of the river. He had an orchard there and with the help of his parishioners managed to eke out a living.

"Why, Sarah, don't you look fine," Al bellowed as he cut the engine and flew out the door, seemingly at the same moment. Mama let him take her hands and spin her around.

After Al had gotten a good look at Mama, he turned toward me. "Laurie girl, you've grown up."

I imagined my dress getting shorter and tighter and exposing me to Nathan's searching eyes.

Nathan laughed softly. There he was, bigger than life, his sandy hair ruffled a bit and his soft gray eyes, the color of a mourning dove's wings, gleaming at me.

I turned to see Star standing on the porch. She was smiling her stupid, all-knowing smile. She turned and went inside.

"Missed you, Laurie," Nathan said as he walked over to me.

I turned to Mama for some help with the conversation, but she was walking toward the house with Nannie and Al.

"Did you?" I asked.

Nathan smiled again. "You're supposed to say you missed me too."

"I did miss you. I missed everyone . . ."

"Learn a lot of city ways?"

"A few," I admitted.

"Ride on a train?"

"Yes."

"In a taxi?"

17

"Yes."

"See the ocean?"

"Some of it."

"Take a boat out on the waves?"

"It made me sick."

Nathan kicked at the dirt. "I got your postcard."

"Good."

"Sorry I didn't write back."

"That's okay."

Al called from the porch, "Nathan, you want to ride over to the singing with Laurie and Sarah? I need to get back home and pick up your ma."

Nathan shouted, "That'd be nice."

I smiled.

Nathan walked over and stroked the automobile. "What a fine piece of machinery! Never seen anything quite so, quite so . . . yellow!"

The singing was held at the Community Building beside the picnic grounds in Guthrie. Before Mama and I went to New York, folks used to take turns having it in the different churches in town; but, as the preachers changed with the seasons, so did the rules.

The Methodists didn't want any hip swaying. The Baptists didn't want any clapping. And the Holiness Set-Aside Saints didn't want any body movement at all, at least not on singing night. They saved their strength for a free-for-all on Sunday morning.

The singing now began at seven o'clock and could last until one o'clock in the morning, depending on how many people wanted to perform. This night there were nearly twenty automobiles and trucks parked beside the Community Building. There was also a scattering of buggies, saddle horses, and

18

one old mule used by Doc Pritchard on his rounds on the back roads.

I sat in the back of the Packard squished between Nathan and Star, feeling something like a sardine in a rolltop can. Star kept scooting against me to make me scoot against Nathan. It was all I could do to hold my ground. After Mama stopped the auto and helped Nannie out, I gave Star the shove she deserved out onto the rock driveway.

"Hey!" Star yelled as she caught her balance. "What you doin'?"

I ignored her and got out of the automobile the best I could with Nathan breathing down my neck.

While Star and Nathan stood and talked to each other, I retrieved my guitar from the tiny space behind the back seat.

Mama looped her arm through mine and caught Star by the elbow on the way to the Community Building. "Let's have us some fun, girls," she said, happier than I'd seen her in a long time.

Nannie called to us, "I'll need a little help with the boarders. Mr. Avartoz and the others should be here any minute."

"You two go ahead," Star said. "Folks are waiting to see you. I'll help Nan."

"We'll wait on you," I said.

Star said, "Go on. It will take us awhile to get everyone inside."

But Nathan went to Star and said, "Go on in. I'll help."

Star started to say something, but, instead, smiled and hurried toward Mama and me.

Star said, "The whole town is waiting to hear the two of you sing. Between Nan and Aunt Nola everyone knows you've taken guitar lessons and voice lessons and —"

"If I remember," Mama started, "we used to be a trio."

19

"I haven't sung since you left," Star said to her feet. "I expect you have a lot of city ways I wouldn't begin to know about. You've probably sung your songs to the best of people."

Mama said, "We have learned some fast licks on the guitar, haven't we, Laurie? But nothing you can't catch up with." She hurried up the stairs.

I wanted to tell Star about my music in New York. About how lonely I had been when I practiced. About how no one up there liked anything I sang or played. About how they said it came from the hills and didn't even have a decent tune, but I couldn't find the words.

We followed Mama inside. The air was thickened by the musty past. Music had filled every crack in the worn clapboard and the thick parquet floor and the hodgepodge of old chairs and pews and stools; and it was stuck there, wedged in memory.

The hair on my arms lifted, and a tingling sensation rose up my back. I loved the place. I loved the sounds made there. The sweet, hollow sounds that came from people's hearts.

Nathan's mother, Marcy, was already there, seated in the front pew. She waved at us, and we walked toward her.

"Nice to see you all home," she said. Her hair and skin reminded me of a sun-ripened peach.

"It's nice to be back," I said.

Mama nodded and excused herself to the other side of the room.

"Sarah has never liked me much," Marcy said, mostly to herself.

Star followed Mama.

"I'm sorry for talking about your mama behind her back, Laurie," Marcy said. She smiled. "Did you have a nice time in New York?"

20

"Nice enough," I said, wondering if I should sit down beside Marcy or go to Mama and Star. Nathan answered the question for me when he came inside and walked over to us, sitting down in the pew beside his mother and motioning for me to sit down beside him.

We were barely settled before Hiram Lawson appeared at the front of the room, preparing to slap his fiddle against his shoulder and get the music started. Hiram played "Arkansas Traveler," "Mandy Lockett," and "Turkey in the Straw," before he gave up the stage, saying, "Sarah and Laurie are back. 'Spect they have a song just about to pop out." He motioned for us to come up. I picked up my guitar and went with Mama to stand beside him. She motioned for Star to join us. Star glanced at Nannie before she slowly walked up to stand beside Mama.

Star whispered, "Sarah, what are we going to sing?"

Mama said, "We're going to start with a little song Laurie wrote for Nan. After that, we'll sing some of the old tunes you know."

Star said, "Okay," and stood quietly, rocking back and forth nervously.

Mama, on the other hand, was about as far from nervous as a being could get. She was on stage. It didn't matter that the stage was in Guthrie, Arkansas, or that most of the audience couldn't carry a tune in a bucket. It was show time.

"We're happy to be back," Mama said to the people.

It was a lie told before God and everyone. I saw Nannie's reaction to what Mama had said. She puckered up like a prune and slid into a seat beside Apples.

Mama started to say something more, but Mrs. Turner, seated at the front, said, "Sing us a purty one, Sarah, honey. Sarah, sing us a purty one, honey."

Suddenly, Mama turned to me and said, "It's stuffy in here.

21

I think I'll get some air. You can sing your little song by yourself." She left then, winding her way through the crowd. Star followed her out and left me on stage with only my guitar for company. It felt strangely familiar.

Hiram nodded at me, so I said, "This is a song I wrote for Nannie called 'She Was A Fine One.'" I strummed the guitar and let Hiram tune his fiddle to it. With a stroke of the strings I sang:

> "Was she a fine one?
> She was the finest.
> Was she the fairest?
> Oh, she was fair.
>
> And did she love you?
> Oh, yes, she loved me.
> Will she be waiting?
> Waiting for me there."

It was home. The sounds of sweet, simple music. The smell of honeysuckle on the breeze. The humming of the people. Then, as if everyone had turned to hear a whispered secret, the crowd's attention was drawn to the front door.

There stood Harvey Brown, the mayor; and Floyd Roth, the schoolteacher. Between them was a strange man dressed in as fine a suit as I had seen in the city. He was puffing on a big cigar and looking over the crowd.

The mayor directed the people to clear a path for them to the front, and I stepped aside with a missed chord. The stranger walked forward and coughed.

"This is Walter Weeks," the mayor said. "He has something to tell you."

Mr. Weeks ran his hands along his lapels. "I have come here to offer you people a proposition you will not want to refuse."

There was silence.

"An opportunity to make money. A shoe factory right here in Guthrie. Jobs. Many jobs. And in a time when jobs are scarce. Money. Good money. Plenty of money for busy hands."

As the whispered secret turned to a blessing the people began to giggle like children. Children given three wishes. In a moment's notice a stranger had turned all the townspeople of Guthrie into babbling elves.

"A shoe factory," was on every lip. People were holding hands and jumping about. Everyone seemed to be happy, too happy to stay put. The crowd slipped out the door.

I put my guitar in the Packard and helped Nannie load the boarders into Mr. Avartoz's automobile. They were upset that the evening had been so short when they had put such effort into getting to the singing. I left Nannie to comfort them and hurried to find Mama and Star.

They were sitting by the well, talking. I heard Mama say, "She can't take another boarder. She just can't."

Star said through tears, "I can't work any harder. She thinks I'm lazy as it is. I'm eighteen. I need to have a little fun."

Mama said, "That's right, you do, honey."

Star blew her nose. I moved toward them, and Mama stood up.

"Did you hear about the shoe factory?" I asked.

"Ten people have told us," Star said, blubbering.

Mama said, "Sounds like the best news Guthrie has had in a long while."

23

"But it'll *change* things," I said.

Mama and Star both looked at me as if I were insane for not wanting things to be different.

"Change would do a lot of people around here a world of good," Mama said as she walked toward the Packard.

Star wiped her face on her sleeve.

"Is there anything I can do for you?" I asked.

Star said no.

I smiled to cover the hurt I felt, knowing Star would rather cry on Mama's shoulder than mine. After all, hadn't they shared their lives through letters while we were in New York? And hadn't Star said she liked Mama's stories better than mine?

"We'd better hurry. Nannie is probably waiting on us," I said.

Star said, "Go on and tell her I'm coming. I need to wash my face. I don't want Nan to see me looking like this."

There seemed to be a lot of crying Nannie had missed.

3

Mama got up at dawn on Saturday and drove her Packard into Harrisburg. Nannie and I stood on the front steps and listened until the last drone of the engine faded into the sounds of the farm waking up.

"She'll be home before supper," Nannie said as much to herself as to me.

I didn't know. Mama had acted sad ever since the singing. It was as if my good memories were her bad ones. "I think she wants to be in California with her friends," I said.

Nannie sighed. "I expect if your mama wants to be in California, she'll find a way to get there."

"I'd rather stay here," I said. The whimper in my voice made me feel ashamed.

Nannie didn't say anything, but she laid her hand on my shoulder before she turned to go into the house.

We had hotcakes and sausage for breakfast. Star tugged at my sleeve and whispered, "Let's have our meal on the back porch, away from everyone."

I followed Star outside and sat on the step beside her.

Between bites of hotcake, Star said, "I just hate the way Apples drizzles syrup over her cakes. And then there's the way Mrs. Turner smothers her sausage with the molasses. Uck! They turn my stomach the way they roll the food around in their mouths, trying to find a tooth to chew with."

"I expect we'll be old someday," I said.

25

Star stopped eating for a moment and looked away. "Even when I'm old I won't end up in a place like this."

"Nannie takes good care of everyone —"

Star pointed her fork at me. "Not by herself, she doesn't."

"I'll help you. That is, if Mama stays."

"What makes you think she won't?" Star asked quickly.

"She's already gone into Harrisburg. Seems the farm drives her crazy or something."

Star plopped her plate on the step. "Sarah left this morning? Why didn't anyone tell me? I would've liked to have gone with her."

"I didn't know she was going —"

"No one tells me anything," Star said. She got up and hurried inside.

I couldn't figure out why Star felt she was the one slighted by Mama's quick disappearance, especially since Mama didn't tell *me* she was leaving until she was in the Packard.

I set our plates on the table beside the door and hurried out to the chicken house to gather the eggs. By the time I finished outside, breakfast was over and Apples was standing at the old tin sink in the kitchen, washing the dishes with Star's reluctant help.

"Where's Nannie?" I asked.

Star didn't look up from the suds as she answered, "Still on her run."

Running around the farm was another of Nannie's peculiarities. Every morning after breakfast she pulled on her old brogans, ate an apple, swallowed a dose of vinegar, and ran five miles around the farm. She would have a cup of thick coffee while she "caught her breath," and then begin a full workday that would weary a strong man to his grave.

When I saw Nannie coming, I got her a cup of coffee and met her on the porch.

26

"Thank you," Nannie said as she took the cup from me and plopped into Apples's rocker. She took a long drink, handed me the cup, and unlaced her shoes.

I knelt down and pulled off her brogans.

"Getting old, child," Nannie said. "Can't run like I used to. Wear out coming through the woods. A wolf on my trail couldn't make me run any faster."

"You're not old," I said.

Nannie patted me on the head and took a long breath.

The sound of an automobile coming up the lane drew our attention beyond the yard.

Nannie stood up. "Wonder who that could be at this time of day?"

"Isn't that Mayor Brown?"

Nannie said, "I believe it is," as she stepped off the porch and walked to where the mayor was parking his automobile.

"What can I do for you, Harvey?" Nannie asked. "Surely you didn't come all the way out here for a cup of coffee?"

Mr. Roth, the teacher, got out with Mayor Brown and walked toward Nannie.

"You still have that summer house on the river, Nan?" the mayor asked.

"Yes," Nannie said. "Why?"

"We've been looking for a suitable place for Mr. Weeks and his family to stay while we're finalizing the building plans for the shoe factory," he said.

"What about Miss Franklin's at Harrisburg? Doesn't she still take boarders?" Nannie asked.

"We think Mr. Weeks ought to be a little closer to the community than Harrisburg. And he'll need a house for his family, not just a couple of rooms," Mayor Brown answered.

Nannie wriggled her toes and rocked back and forth. "My place at the river needs some work. There are holes in the

27

porch screens. The pump needs repairs. And, of course, it needs a good cleaning."

"We have money to cover those expenses," the mayor said. "How long would it take to get it cleaned up?"

"A week — if I can get the materials and workers," Nannie said.

"Perfect," Mr. Roth said. "The Weekses won't have to room and board for very long at all."

"That's the other matter," Mayor Brown said. "The Weekses will be here no later than Tuesday. Think you could put them up until the river house is ready?"

Nannie smiled. "You looking to hire me?"

"You're the finest cook in the county," the mayor said. "We want the Weekses to have the very best."

"And you're willing to pay?"

He smiled. "Name your price."

"How many in the family?" Nannie asked.

"Mr. Weeks, his wife, and three children. Two mostly grown kids and a little fellow."

"Five dollars a day," Nannie said flatly.

The mayor gasped. "That's robbery."

"That's a fair price," Nannie said.

The mayor and Mr. Roth stepped aside and talked for a few moments. When they came back to Nannie, the mayor said, "Your price, then. We want things to be just right. We all need this factory. It will bring new life to Guthrie."

As they drove away Nannie said, "Don't see much wrong with the old life."

"So much for a quiet summer," I said.

Nannie put her arm around me and used me as a crutch to get up the stairs to the porch. "Need to find me a topnotch carpenter."

"Uh-huh," I agreed.

"Need to find me a couple of girls with strong, young legs to go down to the river house and do some cleaning."

"Do we get paid?" I asked quickly.

Nannie answered, "Room and board."

It was a thankless life. I knew Star would agree with me.

They came to eat with Nannie every Sunday noon, scurrying like ants late to a picnic. By "they," I mean Aunt Nola and cousins Peter, Cora, and Bo-Henry.

We had attended the Methodist church that morning. Even Mama had gone with us instead of listening to Al Graham at the Baptist church because the Methodists had a guest speaker, and Nannie said there would be some good singing. There wasn't. Two plump women from Harrisburg sang a duet. They were off-key.

Aunt Nola and her brood had been to the fire-baptized meeting of the Holiness Set-Aside Saints. They handled snakes in their services. At least, I'd heard that. Nannie forbid us to attend church with Aunt Nola on "snake" day.

I saw them walking across the field toward the house. Aunt Nola was in front, holding up her long blue skirt as she stepped over the high fescue, singing at the top of her lungs. Cora was right behind her, walking with her head held high. Bo-Henry was following Cora, and Peter brought up the rear. He was marching with his long arms swinging like twin pendulums on a grandfather clock.

Star walked out beside me on the porch and took a long look at the approaching parade. She turned toward the kitchen and announced, "The locusts are about to swarm."

Nannie stepped to the door and took a swing at Star with a wet tea towel. Star ducked deftly and said, "Cora is impossible," before she went inside at Nannie's insistence.

"Nan, you shouldn't be so hard on Star for lashing out at

29

Cora once in a while," Mama said to defend her sister as she scooted the leaves into the table to make room for the guests. "Her holier-than-thou attitude, though I know it's been taught to her, would get on anyone's nerves."

Nannie slipped the lace cloth over the table. "Don't you girls start in on Nola and Cora. It's not right. Not on a Sunday. Let's have a happy time of it."

"I don't know why you go to all this trouble for *them*," Star said as she poured milk into tall glasses.

"They're family," Nannie said firmly.

"You wait on Aunt Nola hand and foot, and she never does a blasted thing for you," Mama added.

Nannie set down the pan of hot rolls she was carrying and put her hands on her hips. "I don't know where you learned to talk that way. And for your information, young lady, it is *pleasure* to serve family."

"Every Sunday?" Star asked.

"Especially on Sunday. Jesus told us all to be servants. Why, He even washed his disciples' feet." Nannie turned away as if she had scored the final point in the game.

Star whispered to me, "Jesus didn't have to eat lunch with Aunt Nola."

If Nannie had been an apple tree, Star would have been the fruit that fell the farthest from it. They didn't think alike, and I knew it hurt Star that they didn't.

Aunt Nola hit the screen door in a dead sweat. She was panting and wiping her forehead and leaning against the wash cabinet on the porch. "Hallelujah!" she cried. "We certainly had good services today. The Holy Spirit was in us all."

Star whispered, "If you ask me, it looks as if the Holy Spirit nearly did her in."

30

Aunt Nola grabbed a towel in the kitchen and blotted away the sweat on her face.

"Good services, you say?" Nannie asked as she stopped to look at her sister.

"Wonderful," Aunt Nola said, rolling her big green eyes toward Heaven. "Marion Barker got the spirit."

"Better than what she got last year," Star said.

Aunt Nola turned quickly and stared at Star. "What do you mean, better than what she got last year?"

Star smiled. "Last year she only got six weeks in jail for making gin."

Aunt Nola grabbed at her chest. "Nan, Nan, how you have been given such a burden with this girl."

Nannie pointed to Star's chair, and, wisely, Star sat down.

Cora came in from the back porch, smiling. It was plain that she had heard it all. She glanced at Star, then looked at me. "Welcome back, Laurie."

"Thank you," I said.

"Welcome back, Sarah," Cora said.

Mama smiled and turned away.

Cora pooched out her breasts as Star had said she would. The tiny, pearl buttons on her blouse nearly popped from the pressure.

"Smells good," Peter said as he took his place at the table. If things were as they had been when I left Guthrie, those were the only words he would say until his stomach was full.

Bo-Henry hurried to Nannie and put his arms securely around her. Nannie didn't pull away or say anything. She just stood there until Bo-Henry silently let her go and sat down beside Aunt Nola at the table. Bo-Henry was nearly fourteen, but he was small for his age and, as Aunt Nola preferred to say, simple and innocent.

Mr. Avartoz herded the boarders to their places at the far end of the table. They were unusually quiet, the way they always were when Aunt Nola was eating with us. It was as if they were afraid they might say something that might damn them to Hell.

Only Mr. Avartoz dared to speak to Aunt Nola as if he had every right to be eating at the table. I suspected it was because he felt that, since he was Jewish, he had closer ties to God.

After the prayer Nannie said, "Harvey Brown stopped by and asked me to fix up the river house for the Weekses."

Aunt Nola nearly choked on her bite of salad. "Guess you'll be first in line for the jobs." She glanced at Mama.

"Don't plan on it," Nannie said. "What I am planning on is needing someone to look after the repair work at the river house. Think you might be able to see to that, Peter?"

Peter kept chewing. He had always made it a point to avoid work whenever possible.

"Are you busy putting in the field of corn you started on last week?" Nannie asked Peter.

Peter swallowed and looked at Aunt Nola as if he knew she would answer for him.

Aunt Nola said quickly, "We're not putting out that piece of land. It has never been much good anyway. With the shoe factory coming, Peter was planning on getting him a regular lunch-bucket job."

Peter nodded and continued to eat.

Nannie took a bite of food, chewed it slowly, and swallowed it before she said, "I'm not so sure I'd put all my eggs in one basket."

"What do you mean?" Aunt Nola asked, with a humphing sound.

"What if no one wants to buy shoes made on a machine?

Folks have been having their shoes made to order over at Tanyard Springs for years," Nannie said.

"Weeks plans to sell them back East," Aunt Nola spurted.

"What if there aren't many jobs? And if there are jobs, what if they don't pay much?" Nannie continued.

Peter broke all rules when he said through a stuffed mouth, "Heard tell there's going to be sixty-five jobs. Heard tell Weeks is paying one hundred dollars a month. Heard tell heads of families get first pick of the work. Then widows needing an income. Then young men fixing to start families. Right Christian."

"So you're not planting corn?" Nannie asked.

Aunt Nola said, "We'll buy our feed."

Mama looked first at Aunt Nola and then at Nannie. "Seems like the whole town is anxious for *change*," Mama said to Nannie. "Seems like making shoes would be a pretty fine way to make a living compared to the way some people have to make a living now." She glanced at the boarders.

As if they were ordered, the boarders got up and left the room, leaving food on their plates.

"Don't you go scaring them, Sarah girl," Mr. Avartoz said to Mama. He didn't speak unkindly, but with the authority of someone who was usually right.

Nannie said, "I've run this boardinghouse for fifteen years. It has made me a good living. A *good* living. I've helped a lot of people. Taken the burden off of them —"

Mama said softly, "And put it on us."

"What did you say, Sarah?" Nannie asked.

"Nothing," Mama said.

Star smiled at Mama. I knew she had heard what had been said, as I had, but I didn't like Mama speaking unkindly about Nannie.

That was all that was said about the factory and the new jobs. The conversation turned to church and the Holy Spirit and to whose son had run off to the city. Cora and Star and I took our blackberry cobbler out to the front porch to eat.

I knew Star wouldn't have joined us if Nannie hadn't been giving her the "evil eye."

"I'm going to buy me a pair of patent leather shoes with Peter's first paycheck," Cora said wistfully.

"They pinch," Star said.

"Just how would you know?" Cora asked.

Star set down her cobbler and said, "Tried on a pair in Fort Smith."

"You've never been to Fort Smith," Cora spat.

"Guess I have."

"Guess you're a liar."

Star smirked. "You think I'm going to tell you, cousin, how I got to Fort Smith so you can run on your knobby little legs in to Nan and spill your guts about it?"

"You are so vulgar!" Cora screamed. "You are such a vulgar, stupid girl."

"Thank you," Star said as she went into the house.

"I hate her," Cora said to me. She finished her cobbler and stared across the front yard.

I didn't say anything.

Cora said, "I know you love Star. She's your aunt and all, but I don't know how you live in the same house with her. And you're so different, Laurie. Why, if Star had just an ounce of your niceness she might be bearable."

"Thanks," I said, surprised at the compliment.

"Then, again, you've had your moments of meanness," Cora added.

"Come sing for us, Laurie," Nannie called from the parlor.

I got up. I could sing only hymns because Aunt Nola was

34

there, but I'd be singing. I hurried upstairs to get my guitar. Star was there, standing outside my room and leaning against the wall.

"Going to sing?" she asked.

"Come and join me," I said.

"Is Cora still here?"

"She's in the parlor."

"Where's Sarah?"

I motioned toward the backyard. "I saw her walking across the meadow. Guess she had about all of Aunt Nola she could take."

Star pushed by me. "If I hurry I can catch up to her."

I walked downstairs, knowing Star could never hurry fast enough to catch up with Mama. Mama had ways of making her own head starts.

4

The next morning Mama went with Mr. Avartoz to take Ezra to the clinic at Bucks Point. Ezra's legs had been bothering him. Ezra said he had the "rheumatiz," but I could tell by the worried way Nannie acted that she expected the doctor to say it was an ailment that was much worse than merely a "cold" settling in Ezra's old bones.

Star and I went with Peter to work at the river house. It took us most of the day, but we got back to the farm in time to see a new Ford pull up to the house. The driver managed to bump into a flower box as he parked the auto beside the walk.

From the hats of the passengers in the Ford I knew the Weekses had arrived. No one in our part of the woods would have worn hats like theirs. Mr. Weeks had on a hat that was flat on top with a wide purple ribbon around it. Mrs. Weeks had on a red hat that was as cone-shaped as a dunce cap. She popped open her door and squealed, "If this isn't the prettiest place on the face of the earth!"

Star walked toward them and said, deadpan, "No need to unpack. This isn't your stop."

I don't know what Star was thinking. I could tell this brood wasn't about to camp out by the river without running water or a spark of electricity.

Before Mrs. Weeks could answer, Nannie was on the porch saying, "Oh, yes, this is your stop. At least for a couple of days, until our workers get the river house all spic-and-span for you."

Star smirked.

Nannie looked at Star and me and said, "Girls, help the Weekses take their bags upstairs."

"To where?" Star asked quickly.

"To your room. To Laurie's room. To Sarah's room," Nannie said.

"And where do *we* sleep?" Star asked.

Nannie led Mrs. Weeks to the house as she spoke to Star over her shoulder, "Sarah can sleep with me. You and Laurie will sleep in the attic for a couple of nights. It won't kill you."

Star and I looked at each other. We knew a night in the attic *could* kill us. There were bats up there. Bats with fangs and horrible histories of murder. With terror in her eyes, Star told me, "Bats sucked a cow dry at the Wilson's last year. Drier than a desert."

I didn't have time to comment. A fat boy dressed in knickers shoved a suitcase at me. I shoved it back.

Star said, "Seems you're plenty big enough to carry your own bags upstairs."

The boy stood up tall, taller than Star. "Expect I have other things to carry, like my little brother here." A smaller boy crawled out of the automobile. He was at least five years old and seemed perfectly able to walk on his own two feet.

"I'm Lester," the big boy said. "This is Roy Gene. We call him Rah-Rah."

They were two of the homeliest boys I had ever seen. Uglier than Tommy Pickens. Tommy had a face full of warts. Rumor was that a frog had peed on him in his cradle. Frog pee couldn't have hurt these two.

Star took the bag from Lester and watched him carry Rah-Rah into the house. When they were out of sight she made

37

gagging sounds. Before she could say anything, another person got out of the auto. I would like to have said it was another ugly brother, but it wasn't. It was a girl, and she was the furthest thing from ugly I had ever seen.

This new enemy was blond-haired and blue-eyed and tall, and dressed as if she had fallen out of a fashion magazine.

"Hi," she said with a lilt to her voice that sounded like a robin singing.

Star was staring. Now Star shouldn't have been threatened that much by a pretty girl. Star wasn't bad-looking. And she was very likable, until she talked.

I was the one who felt the buzzards swarming over my suddenly inadequate body. People occasionally said I was pretty, but they were tweaking my cheek while they said it. That wasn't the kind of pretty I wanted to be. I wanted to be so pretty that when I got out of an automobile in some strangers' yard they would stand there like complete idiots with their tongues hanging out as they sized me up.

"I'm Betty," the girl said with her musical voice.

"I'm Star," came the reply with the voice of a bullfrog.

"And I'm Laurie," I said. Star nearly choked at the sound of my voice. I had tried to make it soft and sweet, but it came out tense and thin.

"Castor oil would cure that," Star said after Betty had gone into the house.

"We have problems," I said.

Star leaned on the automobile. "And she looks that way after a long ride. Imagine what she will look like after a good night's rest, a bath, and a fresh dress."

"God loves some people more than others."

Star sighed. "Seems that way." She picked up a bag and handed it to me before she got another one for herself. We

38

went inside and set them beside the parlor, where Nannie was serving the Weekses raisin cookies and lemonade.

Nannie said, "Girls, Peter set your cleaning supplies on the back porch. Get them and straighten the attic before supper."

Star stomped on ahead, so I said, "Yes, Nannie."

We found the door to the attic was stuck. Star pounded against it with a broom until it popped open and drew us up the tiny stairs on a hot puff of air.

"I think I'd rather stay at the river house," Star said as she swung the broom at a low cobweb.

"Bugs out there," I said.

"Giant Weeks bugs in here." Star continued to do battle with the spiders.

I moved old furniture to the side and dusted off the ancient bed. "Guess Nannie will give us a mattress."

"Don't count on it," Star said as she sat down on the window seat and looked across the valley.

I sat down beside her. "You can see all you need to see from here. The river. The town. The farms beyond the crossing."

"Is that all that's out there?" Star asked.

"No, it isn't." I got up and continued to work.

Star spoke softly, "Did you like the city, Laurie?"

"It was busy. Very busy."

"I'll bet it was wonderful." Star cupped her face in her hands.

"It was lonely," I said.

"No!"

"Yes. Yes, it was." I could feel a strange relief coming over me, as if I had needed to tell Star how awful it had been in New York.

"Lonely? How could you be lonely with all those people around you?" Star asked, amazed.

"Well, you wrote me about how lonely you were here with Mama and me away. And you had all the boarders around you."

Star sat up. "That's different. They're *old* people. Old people with their lives over. Old people with no hope, no future."

"You really do hate it here at the farm," I said.

Star nodded that it was true. "I couldn't be any worse off if I lived with the undertaker."

"You have Nannie, who loves you. And people to look out for you. And a place . . . a place of your own to feel secure in. It's not like living in an apartment that belongs to someone else. It's not like smelling food someone you don't know is cooking. Everyone knows you here in Guthrie. When you walk down the street they wave or smile or call out hello."

"None of that should matter to you," Star said as if she were excusing herself for not realizing the good things she had.

"What do you mean that it shouldn't matter to me?"

"You're going to sing."

"Sing where?"

"Anywhere Sarah can get someone to listen to you," Star said. She looked at her hands for a moment. "'Course I wasn't supposed to tell. And Nan doesn't know. Your mama is taking you on the road."

"Why?"

"Don't be a goose! You're special, and you know it. Everyone has always wanted to hear you sing ever since you were three years old and Sarah lifted you onto the stage at the Community Building. The audience applauded for you for fifteen minutes."

"They applauded because I raised my skirt and showed off the ruffled panties Nannie had made for me."

"They applauded because you're going to be a star." She again sat back and stared out the window. "Your mama named me Star, but you're going to be the one who gets to be one."

A star? And Mama thought I could be one? This was all a surprise. I hadn't felt as happy since I was seven years old and Nannie let me climb the ladder and place the angel on top of the Christmas tree all by myself. It was a feeling I could get used to.

Star sighed. "You'll be leaving — soon."

There was a pang in my stomach. Why did there always have to be a bad side to happiness? I loved the farm. I didn't want to leave. The corn would be ripening in July, followed by the peaches in August, and later by the fat, red apples in September.

I looked long at Star.

Star said, "You're staring at me."

"Sorry."

She smiled. "Think I'm pretty?"

"Yes."

"As pretty as old Betty Weeks?"

"Pretty as Betty."

Star sat back and continued to stare outside. I cleaned the room and let her dream, knowing dreams were important. I had a new dream of my own to think about — a dream about being a star.

It was after supper when Nathan came by. It was the first time he had called on me since I had been back. I looked a mess. My old dungarees were faded and my shirt was dirty and my hair was in pigtails.

Nathan wanted to go inside, but I insisted we sit on the back porch to have lemonade. Star had convinced me that inside was a sweet dream I should want him to miss. I wouldn't have admitted it, even to Star, but I hoped Betty was tired and had gone on to bed. When there was no sign of her after an hour, I suspected I had gotten my wish.

Then Nannie ruined it all by coming outside and saying, "Nathan, would you mind helping Star and Laurie carry a mattress to the attic?"

Nathan flashed me a questioning look, but I simply shrugged.

We got the mattress from the storage room on the third floor and fought it up the narrow stairs to our bed frame.

"What are you girls doing up here?" Nathan asked.

Star glanced out the window. "We have *guests*. The holy family is visiting. God Weeks, his blessed wife, and the three troll apostles."

"Thought they were staying at the river house," Nathan said.

I answered, "They will be, but things aren't fixed there yet."

Nathan must have sensed we wouldn't have any more time alone. Or maybe he felt out of place in our bedroom. He excused himself with a cough and headed out the door. I followed him into the hallway downstairs. There was a light turned on there. It cast a glow over his head like a halo. He looked absolutely handsome.

Then the worst possible thing in the world happened. The door to Betty Weeks's bedroom floated open and she stepped into that same golden glow dressed in a white wrap thick with pale blue brocade.

"This is Betty Weeks," I said to the back of Nathan's head.

"I'm Nathan Graham," he said to her. He was nearly trembling with excitement.

No, it was my imagination. He couldn't be trembling at the vision of this perfect golden lovely standing not more than three feet from him.

Betty said her favorite word, "hi," and excused herself back into her lair.

Star had caught up with us by then. She didn't say anything as we watched Nathan drift down the stairs on a cloud. After he had gone, she reached into a crock on the hall table and got an apple. Through a big bite of it, she said, "I suppose he knows now that Betty isn't a troll."

On Tuesday Mama and Mr. Avartoz took Ezra back to the doctor at Buck's Point for a treatment. He had polio. It didn't look as if it was going to do much more than annoy him, but Nannie insisted that he have the best care.

Star had begged to go with them, but Nannie convinced her that with the Weekses visiting she was needed to help out even more than usual.

It was late at night, in bed, before Star and I had the chance to be together again. The entire day was spent revolving around the Weekses, as if they were royalty. All of them were demanding, except Betty. She was all sweetness and light. Ready to help. Never asking for anything. It was disgusting.

Star kicked the sheet down to the end of the bed. "I think Betty is a fake."

"Think so?" I asked as I reached down to retrieve my side of the covers.

"No one could be that thoughtful. That perfect. She has all the boarders eating out of her hand. And that's old blood. Think about what she'll be able to do with fresh, hot, young blood."

"The way you say it, makes it sound as if every boy in the county is boiling over."

Star pulled herself up and leaned on one elbow to look at me. "They are. They really are. With a full moon like tonight they are pacing and howling and —"

"You know this for a fact?"

"A fact. Why, Nathan is probably rolling in his covers and calling out *your* name."

"You are the silliest thing."

Star lay back. "Unless he's calling out for Betty."

The words hurt, and I felt tears fill my eyes.

Star must have sensed my feelings because she said, "Only fooling around."

I was thinking of something to say and wondering if I would whimper when I spoke, when a soft pitter-patter crossed the roof.

"Hear that?" Star whispered.

"Probably squirrels," I said.

"Hundred-pound squirrels?" Star asked softly. She sat up and slid off the bed.

"What are you doing?" I asked, apparently too loud to suit her because she made a shushing sound.

Star stood beside the window for a long moment, staring out into the moonlit night. The glass was open, and the screen was fastened by a wooden clasp at the bottom. With a quick sweep she undid the clasp.

I quietly moved from the bed and tiptoed over beside her. Star stepped back and let me look out. There, poised like a frog on a lily pad, was Lester Weeks, dressed only in his underwear. He was staring right at our window.

Star pulled me aside and whispered, "He's set up his own little peep show. Did you see those spyglasses he has in his hand? Last night I bet he waited until we were asleep, sneaked to the window, and got an eyeful."

"What are we going to do?"

Star glanced around the room. "Is that broom still up here?"

"In the corner."

44

"Get it," she ordered.

I got the broom and returned to the window. "Now what?"

"We're going to teach that fat kid a lesson."

"How?"

"Just lie down on the bed and leave it all to me."

I went back to bed and crawled under the covers. Star leaned the broom against the wall and stood in front of the window. She ran her hands through her hair and sighed loud enough to wake the chickens. "It's so *hot* up here, Laurie. And this window is already wide open." She paused and let the words carry into the yard. "I think I'll sleep in the nude tonight. Nan will never know."

She started to pull off her nightgown and discreetly walked away from the window as she did. When she was out of view she dropped her arms and the gown slid back into place. Then she hurried to the window and picked up the broom.

It was torture after that. The longest minutes in history. There was no noise inside or out, except for the manic hooting of an owl near the barn.

Finally, there was the flutter of the softest footstep. It was aimed toward the window. It was followed by a regular flow of them and the sound of breathing and, could it be, boiling blood.

If I lived to be one hundred and five I would never forget the look on Lester Weeks's face as he approached the window. There was enough moonlight to catch the gleam in his eyes and to see the way his lips were curved upward as if he were thanking all the heavens for his good fortune. Then there was the look of sheer panic as Star's well-aimed broom zipped through the screen and hit him in his soft, pudgy stomach, making the tiniest thudding sound.

At first Lester seemed to be thrown only a step back, but it was enough for him to lose his balance. It was a slow act, like that of a high-wire performer; and I had plenty of time to get a front-row seat beside Star before Lester took his last few steps along the edge of the roof, onto the gutter, and into thin air.

It took him less than a second to fall three stories to the ground. Not until we heard him moan did it even cross my mind we might have done him some sort of permanent harm. Star was holding her sides and letting go with great belly laughs.

"What if he's hurt?" I asked.

Star wiped away tears. "If he is, I hope it's his whatchamacallit."

I grabbed my wrap and hurried downstairs.

Nannie met me in the hallway. "Did you hear that noise?" she asked.

I didn't answer but went on through the kitchen with Nannie following me. It took us a minute to find Lester. He hadn't made it entirely to the ground. He was hung in the middle of the lilac bush beside the porch like a forgotten Christmas tree ornament.

"What happened, son?" Nannie asked innocently.

"I fell," he breathed.

"You fell from where?" Nannie asked.

Lester pointed toward the sky.

"Your room is on the other side of the house," Nannie said, looking up with an amazed expression.

Lester let her help him out of the bush before he answered slowly, "It was a very long fall."

That was all that was said. Lester went inside. Nannie went to her room. I went back to the attic with the laughing idiot. Star kept it up for thirty more minutes. She finally fell asleep with a smile still on her face.

5

The next morning, Lester Weeks hobbled downstairs and sat on the front porch with Ezra and Nehemiah. From the parlor, Star and I could hear him talking loudly with the twins. They were talking about women.

Ezra said with his whispery voice, "I claimed me a little gal along about, let me see, along about 1870. Isn't that right, brother?"

Nehemiah made the groaning sound he always made before he spoke. "Seems it was more toward the eighties."

"She was a good cook," Ezra said.

"Cooking was about all she was good at," Nehemiah added.

Lester mumbled something about how he understood.

"Listen to that," Star whispered to me. "Lester thinks he's a man about town."

As Star spoke, we heard Lester say, "I'm thinking of doing me some claiming too."

"Got you a little filly picked out, have you?" Ezra asked.

Lester said, "Thinking of courting Star."

Nehemiah made his groaning sound.

"What's wrong?" Lester asked.

Ezra said, "You might have bit off a little more than you can chew."

By that time Star was on the porch, standing with her

47

hands on her hips and glaring first at Ezra and then focusing on Lester's suddenly shame-blistered face.

"Guess my intentions are known now," Lester said solemnly to Star. "Should have made them known in private, only to you."

Star poked him in the chest with a long, determined finger. "Your intentions don't mean Old Billy Ned to me. You can *intend* until you turn into a worm. You can *intend* until the roosters lay eggs. You can *intend* —"

"I get it," Lester said loudly, glancing at all of us and having eyes that said he wished we weren't there to hear the rejection.

"You're too . . . you're too —" Star started.

Lester fell to his knees and grabbed Star's hands.

It was apparently all Star could take. With a swift kick she again pushed Lester, this time onto the row of Easter flowers in the garden by the porch. Lester looked like a perfect fool, sitting among the daffodils with his pale round face staring up at us like a weed.

Unfortunately, Nannie came out onto the porch in time to see Lester get up and dust off the seat of his trousers.

"Laurie, what is going on here?" Nannie asked curtly.

I made gestures but was unable to speak.

"It's my doing," Star said. "I pushed his highness off the porch."

"Then apologize this very minute," Nannie said.

"I don't plan on it," Star said.

Ezra and Nehemiah got up then, swaying and holding onto each other. When they were inside Nannie said again, "Apologize this very minute."

Lester tried to speak, but Nannie shushed him.

It was a standoff: Nannie with her hands on her hips and Star with her jaw set.

48

"Sit on the keg under the peach tree until you decide to tell Lester you're sorry," Nannie said sternly.

Star started toward the backyard. She mumbled, "I'll tell him I'm sorry when the Wigerstat freezes in July."

"What did you say?" Nannie asked.

Star said over her shoulder, "I said, 'Yes, ma'am.'"

Star sat on the keg all afternoon, not even getting up to go to the outhouse. I guess along about twilight she figured Nannie wasn't going to bend, so she came out onto the front porch where everyone was seated. Lester was sitting on the steps beside a big pan of popcorn. When he saw Star he hopped up and took a step toward her.

"Sorry for pushing you," Star said quickly.

Before Lester could tell her it was all right, she ran inside and upstairs.

It was after eight o'clock when Nannie said good night to the Weekses, cleaned up the porch, and managed to point the boarders upstairs to their beds.

I fixed Star a glass of cider and took it to the attic, where I found her sitting on the window seat.

"What are you doing? Pouting? I thought you would be in bed," I said.

Star was completely dressed. She was wearing her Sunday shift and her good black oxfords. "I need to get away from here for a while. Thought I'd wait and see if you wanted to come along."

"Where?" I asked.

"Here and there. See some things maybe even *you* haven't seen before."

"Does Nannie know about this?"

Star gave me a piercing look. "Oh, sure. I always wait until late at night and sneak out when Nan knows."

49

"Excuse me for being stupid."

"Are you coming or not?" Star stood up.

"Nannie will come looking and blister us."

"Don't worry about it."

"How are we getting out?" I asked. "And won't I need to get my pink dress?"

"You're not going with me if you wear that dress."

"I bought that dress in New York City. It's what everyone is wearing —"

"You look like the tooth fairy in it," Star said as she reached under the bed and pulled out a box. "Try this on. I wore it a couple years ago."

The dress in the box was navy blue with tiny pearl buttons. It was a fully grown woman's dress, complete with darts for a bosom. I glanced at Star. She seemed to be waiting for a comment she could jump on. "It's pretty," I finally said, hoping my compliment was convincing.

"It's classy," Star corrected. "It was my favorite, but I outgrew it. It can be yours now."

"Thanks." I pulled the dress out of the box.

Star moved toward the window as I dressed.

"We're climbing onto the roof?" I asked. "Remember, Lester fell —"

"We'll walk around the roof and climb down the trellis," Star said as she hoisted one leg out the window and disappeared into the darkness.

I stepped onto the shingles and felt my foot slip. I stood there with my legs spraddled out for what seemed like an eternity before Star came back around the corner and took hold of my hand. At the trellis she had to go down in front of me and let me lean my rear against her shoulder for balance.

"You aren't the most graceful person I've ever known," Star said as we slipped out of the yard.

"I haven't sneaked out before," I said to her as she quickly moved away.

"Just do what I do, and you'll be all right," Star said with a voice that told me she wasn't quite as experienced at this business as she expected me to believe.

We took the short cut across the meadow to the road. It wasn't hard to see. The moon was full, although it looked as if a bank of black clouds could cover it at any moment.

We walked about a quarter of a mile down the road before Star said, "If someone I even halfway know drives by, I'm going to flag down a ride. I'm ruining my shoes on this gravel."

I hoped no one would show, but within five minutes an old truck slid to a stop beside Star.

She stepped on the truck's running board and asked, "You fellas give us a ride to the hollow?"

I heard masculine grumblings as Star waved for me to come on. I peeked inside the cab of the truck to see two boys I couldn't remember having seen before in my entire life.

"This is Alvin Parker and this is Willie Tate," Star said as she pushed me next to Alvin, who was driving.

Both boys nodded.

Star said, "Alvin hasn't lived here very long. His daddy is taking work with the railroad over at Pitcher. You remember Willie, don't you? He lives with his granny at the edge of the swamp."

I gasped, then pretended to cough. Willie's grandmother was known far and wide as a witch of sorts. A soothsayer. A healer. She was tucked away where no one had to look at her unless they wanted to. Here was her flesh and blood breathing the same stale air in the pickup as Star. I couldn't believe it. Star was as superstitious as an undertaker born on Friday the thirteenth in a leap year.

51

"Willie here can be our good luck piece," Star said shakily as if she knew what I was thinking.

A living rabbit's foot. I would have laughed, but the whole scene seemed like something out of a bad dream.

"I had just about given up on you," Willie said to Star. "We've driven past here three times already. But Alvin said to give you a few more minutes, since you were bringing your niece along."

Alvin turned to smile at me, but I turned from him to Star. She had planned all of it. I elbowed her hard.

Willie rattled on, "Me and Alvin have a dollar between us. That's a few brews apiece and something to eat."

I couldn't wait until we reached our destination and Alvin parked the truck, to pull Star aside and ask, "Where have you brought me?"

She patted my cheeks. "To a juke joint. Just some good old boys having a fine time. Nothing more. We'll be back at the farm before sunup."

I took a long look at the place. It was an old house with a sagging roof and boarded-up windows.

Star stepped in front of me, cutting off the view. "What's wrong? Ain't it good enough for you? You get too uppity for your raising and you're liable to regret it."

"Is it good enough for you?" I asked quickly.

The question threw Star. I could tell by the way she rocked back on her heels. "Shoot! I'm just an old country girl, going nowhere, doing nothing special with my life. I might as well make the most of it," she said with a hint of annoyance.

As a last attempt to leave, I said, "They won't let me in. I'm only fifteen."

"They'll let you in. You fill out that dress enough," Star said as she took my hand and pulled me around the truck.

Alvin looped his arm through mine, and we followed Star and Willie into the house that reeked of hard cider and tobacco. The inside of the place was no bigger than Nannie's kitchen and dining room, but there were at least fifty people in there. A man was playing a fiddle under a disconnected stovepipe while two other men, holding guitars, were sitting down as if they were taking a break.

"The party can begin now," Willie said as he pulled Star to the middle of the floor. "Come on, Spencer, you and Luke get off your behinds and strum us some traveling music," Willie insisted.

The two men with the guitars stood up and hit a couple of chords. Then the man with the fiddle pulled out a few long draws and started playing a wild jig.

Star and Willie flew down one side of the floor and back to the middle. Then they pushed into the crowd, grabbed a couple standing by the barrel, and drew them into their frenzied steps. After that everyone seemed to dance.

Alvin was at my side then, holding out a jar full of home brew.

"No, thank you," I said. "I don't drink."

He set the jar down. "Maybe since you're home Star will come out to dance more often. Willie does like her."

"Star isn't a regular?" I asked.

"No, golly gee, no," Alvin said. "Willie has to beg her to come. She slips out now and then, but she's always so afraid someone will find out."

"How did Star meet Willie?"

"Nan takes care of Willie's old grandma from time to time when she's ailing."

"Oh."

Alvin asked, "Want to dance?"

Star and Willie whirled by.

"You've never been to something like this before?" Alvin said when I didn't answer.

"No," I said.

53

He stared into my eyes. "My pa would whup me for even lookin' in the window of a place like this."

I nodded.

"Your pa do the same?"

"My daddy's dead," I said.

"Sorry," Alvin said. "Star didn't tell me the particulars about you."

I watched Star, dancing like a gypsy. She had changed partners at least four times already.

"Everyone likes Star. She's a lot of fun," Alvin said. "Now, how about that dance?"

I was about to accept when Star stepped over to one of the band members and got his guitar from him. "We have a treat, folks," she said teasingly. "My little niece is going to bring us a few tunes she picked up in New York. Imagine that. New York City."

One hundred eyes were suddenly focused on me and my floppy-topped dress — one hundred Rebel eyes staring at a damned Yankee.

I smiled as widely as I could and took the guitar from Star.

"I don't care to sing any of those city songs I learned, but I would like to sing a few tunes that you may know." I started with "Wildwood Flower" and then went into "Blue Tail Fly." The people loved the songs. They hollered and danced around me and said they liked the way I picked.

All the while Star stood against the wall, talking to Willie.

After my third song I gave the guitar back to its lonely owner and walked outside. It was going to rain. The tops of the pines were lit with the quick glow of lightning.

I sat beside the truck for the longest time before Star came out and walked over to me. "So here you are. Aren't you having any fun?"

"It embarrassed me to sing on such short notice as that," I

54

said, not looking up. "It embarrasses me to be in a place like this."

Star didn't say anything.

"I want to go home," I said.

"We have a couple hours more to spare," she said as she sat down beside me.

"Guess I could walk if you're set on staying."

"You aren't going to walk."

"If you don't get our ride out here, I am."

"So that's how it's going to be."

"Yes."

Star stood up and pulled me to my feet. She looked into my eyes, then past me. "I expect you're going to tell Nan I brought you here."

"I've never told on you. Why would I start now?"

"I'll get Willie and Alvin," Star said as she went back inside.

It was a while before the three of them came out to the truck. The storm was continuing to build, and the black clouds were low and moving quickly beneath the weak rind of moon. I heard them talking among themselves, saying words like "baby" and "saint."

The company on the ride to the farm was, to say the least, cool. Maybe even downright cold. But before we got there it warmed up considerably. It started when Alvin parked the truck alongside the road and Willie scooted close to Star and gave her a slurpy kiss right on the mouth.

She pushed him away and said, "Don't you ever do that again without asking me first."

"Seems you owe me a little something," Willie said with the loud voice of liquor.

"I don't owe you a thing," Star insisted. She pushed Willie again.

"I think you do," he said.

55

Star took hold of my hand as if she thought she would have to persuade me to leave. "Let us out of the truck."

Willie said, "No."

"I mean it," Star warned.

"I'll let you out," Alvin said as he opened his door and scooted out.

I slid across the seat, and Star followed, fighting away Willie's demanding hands.

"I ain't gonna take you nowhere more," Willie called out the truck window as Alvin steered it into the night.

Star sat down in the dark on a log. "Thought I was showing you a good time."

"I know," I said as I sat down beside her.

"Thought you liked the attention you get when you sing."

"Sometimes. Not in a honky-tonk. Why did you take me there?"

Star scooted a little closer to me. "I've been jealous of your travels. I guess I wanted you to see that I've done some things, too."

"You don't have to do a thing to impress me," I told her.

Star sighed and looked toward the sky. "It's five miles across the fields to the farm. We're going to get wet."

"Then let's get started," I said.

We had run for only a few minutes when I felt the first fat drops of rain on the top of my head. By the time we reached the deserted barn at the Callihan's old farm, it was raining cats and dogs.

We flew inside and leaned against the wall to catch our breath. "There's a lantern and matches in a barrel over here," Star said as she moved across the floor. She tripped over something and let out a string of curse words I had never heard all in a row before.

"Find them?" I asked.

"Yes," Star said as she lit a match. She touched the match to the wick on the lamp and the whole barn glowed.

"How'd you know that stuff was here?"

Star adjusted the wick on the lamp. "Believe it or not Cousin Cora showed me one evening when we walked home from services. She said she put them there because she likes to slip off sometimes and read."

Together we said, "Imagine that!"

Star moved toward a rickety ladder leading into the loft. "Let's go on up."

I stayed right against her as we climbed up the ladder. What was at the top of the stairs wasn't what I expected. The loft had been swept clean, and there were two old chairs and a small table placed against the back wall. Star walked to the table and ran her hand across it. There was no dust.

"More goes on up here than folks would figure," I said.

"Be a better world if people would mind their own business," Star said.

"I didn't mean anything by that. I wasn't passing judgment on anyone. Nannie says every woman has a little hay in her hair."

"Nan does think she knows it all," Star said, sighing. "It's creepy in here. We should go home, storm or no storm."

I agreed. We climbed down and again ran into the cold, hard rain. It was almost dawn when we reached the back porch. We slipped out of our wet dresses, and Star wadded them up and held them under her arm as she climbed the trellis. Just as I started up, someone opened the back door.

Standing there, in her morning clothes, was Nannie. She put a finger to her lips.

Star, unaware of Nannie, whispered, "Are you coming?"

"I need to go to the outhouse," I answered, still looking at Nannie.

"Well, hurry up and don't get caught," Star said, her voice trailing away as she climbed.

"Have you been out on an adventure?" Nannie asked.

"Yes, ma'am," I breathed.

"Have a good time?"

"No, ma'am." I started to cry. I didn't want to, but the tears came so quickly I couldn't help it.

Nannie slipped a strong arm around me. "Now, don't do that. I certainly don't think any less of you for gallivanting around in the middle of the night. There's lilac on the breeze and all that. I understand."

"Yes, ma'am," I mumbled.

"Laurie, girl, you can't keep your chicks too close to the coop. They won't know how a fox looks if you do. And then when the fox slips up on them they'll run to him with open arms, so to speak. I think it's better to let the chicks peck around the yard a little, get a scare or two, and be all the wiser for it. Do you understand?"

I nodded that I did.

"Let's keep this between you and me," Nannie said as she directed me toward the trellis and gave me a boost up to the first rung.

When she pulled back her hand I climbed with a surety I hadn't felt before, knowing that if I fell Nannie would be there to catch me.

6

The river house was nearly finished by the next Saturday, so Nannie gave a "going-away" party for the Weekses. She invited Aunt Nola and her family, plus the Grahams, to come to eat and stay to listen to Mr. Weeks announce the location of the shoe factory.

Mr. Weeks would make his announcement in our parlor. He would also make the announcement in every other parlor and cowshed and store in the county that had a radio. He was the guest of WOTM, Wonder of the Mountains, radio station in Harrisburg.

WOTM wasn't much of a radio station. It operated out of the top floor of Tyler's Feed and Grain in downtown Harrisburg. It had only a thousand watts and could be heard regularly only over a distance of thirty miles. Avery Tyler, manager and only announcer, advertised for anyone who heard the station's programs at a long distance to write and let the people in the Harrisburg area know that they had. For months the people from the farthest away who heard WOTM were an elderly couple in Springfield, Missouri. After that there had been a letter all the way from Chicago, Illinois, from a local boy who had gone East to make his fortune. There was much speculation at the country stores over that Chicago claim. Most said the boy was so homesick he was probably just hearing the mountain music on the wind.

By the time the supper dishes were washed, everyone had gone into the parlor to listen to the radio. Nannie insisted that the boarders be allowed to find their seats first.

Apples sat beside Mr. Avartoz on the sofa. The Baker twins were asleep on either side of Mrs. Turner, and she was sitting still with a resigned look on her face, as if she were a single volume held up by fragile bookends.

When Mama and Star walked into the parlor, Mama said loud enough to be heard from the bottom of a well, "For once, for once in my life, I would like to have a pick of the seats."

Star's expression said that she agreed.

Apples started to get up, but Mr. Avartoz slipped his hand on her knee and said to Mama, "Sarah, where are your manners?"

Nannie peeked into the parlor then and asked, "What's going on?"

Mama flushed crimson and said, "I'm going out to sit on the porch. Anyone coming with me?"

Star said, "I will."

Mama looked at me.

"Thought I'd listen to the radio, Mama," I said, feeling as if I were being forced to choose sides.

Mama turned and left with Star following at her heels like a puppy.

Betty and Lester slipped into their seats on the floor near the radio. Their parents had left early to go to the feed store to make the announcement; and, to everyone's joy, they had taken Rah-Rah with them.

It was 5:45, a clear fifteen minutes before broadcast time. Everyone sat, speechless, looking at the radio and waiting.

I'd had a radio to myself while Mama and I were in New York. It had been my only friend. The broadcasting there was mostly CBS, and the programs were great. I especially liked the "Morning Merry Makers" on at 9:30 after Mama had gone to work and the "Columbia Club" on at 10:45. Late at night Mama and I would listen to "Dream Boat" and the "Hotel Paramont Orchestra." I learned to sing all the popular songs while being accompanied by the best musicians.

I couldn't imagine what programs would come out of the attic of the feed store. I guess everyone else was thinking about it, too, because Ezra woke up and said, wheezing, "I hope there ain't any of them pianee students beating on the keyboard tonight. Last time that pounding nearly did me in."

Nehemiah made his gasping sound and said with his eyes still closed, "I can take the piano students. It's that whiny Nazarene preacher I can't stand. Sounds like he's talking through a tomato can."

Mr. Avartoz moved Apples aside with a gentlemanly gesture and got up to turn on the radio. It wasn't time for the program yet, but I knew he enjoyed zeroing in on the static after he turned the knob.

After a couple of minutes he turned to everyone and said, "It's almost time for the music."

Nannie jumped up, as if rehearsed, and passed out cider and popcorn.

The music blasted through the radio speakers so loudly when broadcasting began that everyone screamed. Mr. Avartoz fixed the volume. "Sorry for the fright," he said.

After the strains of music Avery Tyler said, "Well, howdy, friends and neighbors. Pull up a chair. Sit a spell. Enjoy our broadcasting for the evening. Three hours of entertainment, news, and general joviality. Our first program is sponsored by the Blakely County Mercantile. It's called 'Melody Time,' and I think you're going to like it. It will feature vocal selections by the Blakely County Women's Glee Club. Here they are."

What followed was beyond description. Nathan's mama

and daddy scooted close to each other on the floor and seemed to be napping as they listened to the first selection. Everyone else sat quietly and didn't show any disapproval of the music, despite its being off-key. They acted as if those ladies were seated in front of them, performing only for their enjoyment.

Since it wasn't "foot-tapping" music, Nannie let us young people go out on the porch until some comedy or something else, anything, came on.

Mama and Star were sitting in the porch swing.

"You all haven't missed much so far," I said to them.

"We heard the glee club," Mama said. "As loud as that radio is cranked up, a person passing by the river could hear it."

Betty said to no one in particular, "Those ladies are doing the best they can. I'm certain of it."

Nathan smiled at her as if she had uttered something really important.

Mama looked long at me. I was feeling really uncomfortable under her stare when she announced, "Laurie can certainly sing better than those women on the radio."

Cora said, "I expect she can."

Nathan smiled and then turned away.

Star said, "I can sing better than those women, and I can't even hum."

Everyone laughed and began to file back inside.

I stayed for a moment and sat beside Mama in the swing. "You want me to sing for a living?" I asked.

"It's not like you couldn't do it. It's nothing you wouldn't like to do, is it?"

"I guess not," I said, wondering why Mama's tone was so tense.

She patted my knee and said softly, "You may be our only way out of here."

I just sat there beside Mama, stunned that she would even consider using me as an excuse to leave home, until Nannie came out and said, "I'm refilling the cider glasses. It's almost time for the announcement."

Mama and I made it to the parlor in time to hear Avery Tyler say, "Tonight we have a special announcement of concern to our neighbors over at Guthrie."

Ezra, Nehemiah, Apples, Mrs. Turner, and Bo-Henry were all fast asleep. The suspense was wasted on them.

All the other adults were sitting up and listening, though. Mr. Weeks came on and sounded as if he knew what he was talking about. He said, "After long deliberation and considerable examination I have decided to build the shoe factory near the swamp on the east side of the dam. There is a place called Hallowed Meadow which has been owned by Miss Rhetta Harper for over forty years. We have secured a deed from Miss Harper, and the building will begin by the end of the summer."

"Near the swamp?" Al Graham questioned.

Mr. Avartoz looked amazed.

Nannie stood up and said, "Why would anyone build anything way out there?"

Star said, "It isn't all that far away. You can see the ridge of hills near the swamp from the front porch."

Nannie left quickly.

Avery Tyler was back on then, saying, "I have a final announcement. The twenty-fourth of this month there will be a talent search in Little Rock. All comers are welcome. There is an entry fee of one dollar. There will be cash prizes. More on this next Friday during the regular broadcast of WOTM."

I heard the announcement for the talent search as if it were broadcast right into my ears. Everyone else was talking about the shoe factory as they filed out of the parlor. Everyone except Mama. She was staring at me again.

"Do you want to go to the talent search?" Mama asked.

I glanced around the parlor. I remembered how I felt placing that angel on the Christmas tree, and I remembered how good it felt to hear applause, even at the juke joint. Softly, I said, "Yes." And I knew it was what Mama had been hoping to hear.

Star appeared at the parlor door. "Nathan is getting ready to leave. You had better tell him good-bye before Betty does." She left in a huff.

I said sheepishly, "Star thinks Betty is moving in on Nathan."

Mama smiled. "There will be other boys besides Nathan." She patted my arm and left.

I turned off the light in the parlor and saw how the radio dials were reflecting the moonlight. I could sing better than those ladies in the glee club. I was certain I could; but maybe Star was right, maybe anyone could sound better than they did.

Star was back at the door then. She said disgustedly, "They're gone. You've missed your only opportunity." She stomped up the stairs.

I took a final look at the radio. No, maybe not. Mama knew it. I knew it. There was at least one other opportunity for me.

The next Friday morning we loaded Peter's truck with some things the Weekses would need at the river house. Their furniture hadn't arrived yet. After their personal things were stowed in their automobile, they all piled in except for Mrs. Weeks. She seemed reluctant to leave. I expected it was because she had become used to Nannie waiting on her, but after she and Nannie had shared a long hug I realized she would miss the company.

After we arrived at the river house Mrs. Weeks refused to get out of their automobile. She got out only after Rah-Rah climbed a tree, and she seemed to be the only one who could persuade him to get down before he broke his stupid neck.

"Now there's an indoor water pump and a nice icebox and a screened porch," Nannie said as she comforted Mrs. Weeks while they walked toward the house.

"I suppose the peace and quiet will be rather pleasant back here," Mrs. Weeks said hesitantly.

"Star and Laurie will bring you anything you need," Nannie said.

Star set a basket of canned goods on the front porch with a thud.

Lester came running toward her. "I would have carried that basket in. You didn't have to pick up anything that heavy."

Star said, "Back off, Lester, or I'll —"

Nannie glanced over her shoulder and gave Star a look that would have dropped a squirrel at a hundred paces.

When Lester saw that Star was going to continue to insult him he turned toward me and asked, "Laurie, are you girls going to the singing tonight?"

I said yes, and Star groaned and got into the truck.

"Star doesn't care for me much, does she?" Lester asked.

"Seems that way," I answered.

"She's what I've been looking for . . . all of my life."

I stepped toward him and said as seriously as I could, "Lester, I'd keep that to myself . . . and live."

I went out to the truck, and Star said through clenched teeth, "Don't say one word."

I went into the parlor that afternoon to practice the songs I was going to sing that night at the Community Building. I had just started playing my guitar when Star came in.

"Nathan is going to pick you up this evening. I arranged it for you," Star said smugly.

"Don't be my matchmaker," I said, pretending to be angry at her meddling.

But that evening I let everyone go to the singing without me and waited for Nathan beside the well on the little rock bench Papa Gabriel had built for Nannie.

Nathan was late, and I could hear him pushing his daddy's truck to new speeds as he drove up Woodcutter Road. He whipped up the lane and parked beside me. He hopped out of the truck and pulled out a metal contraption from the back.

"Is that the radio set Star said you've been building?" I asked.

"Nah. This is my latest invention. I want a quartz for my radio set. It costs five dollars, and I'll have to wait until I get my pay at the end of the apple harvest. I don't want one of those cheap galena crystals nearly everyone settles for," he said.

"What is this invention?" I asked.

Nathan spun a brush. "It's a dishwasher. You put it in the sink, attach it to a little motor, and stand back and wait for scrubbed dishes."

"Nannie would say women have children for that."

"Buying one of these will be easier than having a child," Nathan said with a wise look on his face.

"Did you want to take it inside?"

"Your mama said to leave it on the back porch. We're going to try it out in the morning. Your mama has an eye for progress," he said. After he had secured his invention under the table beside the door, he helped me into the truck.

On the way to the singing, I said, "Surprised you asked me to come with you."

"Why's that?" Nathan asked.

66

"Since you've met Betty, I thought you might ask her."

Nathan patted the steering wheel with his palm. "Girls like her are a dime a dozen."

I smiled, knowing full well if that was true there wouldn't be a single piece of pocket change left in the county.

The dessert tables were arranged under a small grove of white oaks beside the Community Building. Since the eating wouldn't begin until at least nine o'clock, lanterns had been hung in many of the branches. Some men were trying to secure them when Nathan and I arrived.

Nathan went over to help, and I carried my guitar inside to find Mama and Star. I didn't see them, so I settled back to listen to the Henderson family sing. There were eight kids in the family and another one on the way. Mrs. Henderson had made all of them shirts or dresses out of the same blue calico print. They looked real professional, even if their song was a little rusty. When the Hendersons had finished, Martha and Elroy Tinker sang the same duet they performed at every singing they attended.

Bob Watkins, who was serving as master of ceremonies, motioned to me, and when I nodded that I was ready, said, "Now Laurie has a song for us."

I climbed up to the platform and was about to begin when Mama appeared, with Star in tow. Mama yelled, "Just a minute." She escorted Star to the stage.

Star stepped up beside me. She was trembling. We turned away from the crowd for a moment. "I don't want to be up here, Laurie, but I couldn't get Sarah to understand. I'm not like you. I'm not like her," Star said through tears.

I took a long look at Star. I could see she was serious. "Let's make the most of it."

Star quickly wiped her eyes as if she were ashamed to be

crying. "How are we going to do that? I'm so embarrassed being up here."

"Don't worry about being embarrassed. You have talent."

"Go ahead. Rub it in, little miss big-time."

My heart couldn't have hurt any worse if Star had squished it in her hand, but I said, "You are one of the funniest people I know. Let's use it right now. We'll pretend all of this is part of the act. Mama won't tell. She'll be happy you're doing anything."

Star said, "I don't know what you mean."

"I saw vaudeville in New York. Sometimes the singer would just wail away while a comedian would mimic or tell jokes or, well, just be a regular pain."

Star stood up a little taller. "People like that?"

"Pokin' a little fun never hurt anyone, especially these people. They're all great kidders."

"Aunt Nola included?"

"Go ahead, find the oddball," I said as I started to turn around.

Star grabbed me. "You lead. Might as well give your plan a try."

"We'll do the Bridesmans. Find a hat, something to use as a beard, and a pipe," I told her.

Star dropped off the side of the stage and began to rummage in the podium there. Then she spoke to Nathan.

I turned back to the group and began to strum a little background music. I said, "Star and I have decided to bring to you some of your favorite local singers. A tribute of sorts."

Star appeared on stage wearing a brown felt hat pulled down over her eyes and a white beard she had apparently thrown together out of something used at the last community Christmas program. She begged a pipe off old Mr. Langston, who was standing, open-mouthed, beside the stage.

"First, Mr. and Mrs. Bridesman," I said.

The Bridesman family was known for their moonshine. They didn't attend the singing regularly and weren't there that night. Mostly when they performed it was through the thick veil of liquor.

I started, "Ah, ha, ha, you and me, little brown jug, how I love thee."

At that point Star burped loudly. The crowd went wild. We finished that song, and I whispered the next act into Star's ear. She passed the pipe back to Mr. Langston, threw the hat to Nathan, and pulled the cotton up on her head and twirled it into pigtails.

"Next is Molly Harper and Mike Weaver," I announced. Molly and Mike had been "courting" for fifteen years. I sang, "I really love you, darling, I do."

Star bellowed, "And, Mikey, you know I love you, too." She wildly kissed the air and twisted her hair and made little hearts at me.

"I want to marry, Molly, honest I do. So won't you ask me —"

Star interrupted with a loud statement, "Why, Mike, that's up to . . . you!"

I shook my head as if it were news to me.

From the back of the room Mike Weaver shouted, "Well, maybe I *will* ask her, now that's all settled."

Molly leaned against him and smiled. The people loved it. Star was taking bows.

"Let's do another one," I said.

Star, still bowing, said, "Let's quit while we're ahead." She got down from the stage and hurried outside.

Nathan helped me down, and we followed her out.

"That worked out fine," Mama said to me.

"Star can't take the pressure," I said with a voice that was shriller than I intended. "She doesn't like to perform. That's a fact."

Mama didn't say anything more. I knew she was watching me as I walked away. I could feel the stare from her steel gray eyes piercing my back.

The "young people" had a place in the yard we called our own. Most everyone was already there when Nathan and I arrived, including Willie Tate and Alvin Parker.

Star walked over to me and whispered, "I didn't think they would have the nerve to show up at a regular gathering like this, with their reputations, well, you know. Something might be said about the other night. Maybe you'd better get Nathan out of here."

It didn't sound like such a bad idea, and I was about ready to ask Nathan to sit with me on the front steps, but Willie stepped forward and said to Star, "Enjoyed that little skit you did. You should have told me you were taking to the stage. I wouldn't miss a single show."

Star stopped him with, "Let's talk over by the sycamore grove, to ourselves."

Willie let out a low whistle. "You ain't ashamed to be seen with me, are you? We've been out before, haven't we, Shining Star?"

Star blushed.

"Shining Star?" Willie continued. "Isn't that the lovey name you like for me to call you?"

Star said, "Shut up."

"Don't think I will," Willie said.

Alvin pulled at Willie's arm, but Willie knocked him away. The crowd tightened the circle around them. Willie reached out and grabbed Star by the arm. She couldn't shake loose. The first to come to her aid was Wendall Taylor. Wendall was simpleminded and lived with his aged mother at the edge of the deepest woods in the county. He couldn't always think clearly, but he was as big as a bear. Wendall managed to pop Willie in the jaw, which caused Willie to lose his grip on Star.

With a slick step Willie kicked Wendall in the stomach and bowled him over like a hollow tree in a tornado. Before Wendall could get up, Willie kicked him in the face.

"Don't defend my woman," Willie warned Wendall.

Wendall looked up at him with sad eyes. His lips were bleeding onto his chin.

Most of the girls started screaming. Loudest among them was Cousin Cora. You would have thought she had never seen blood before. She was hopping up and down and calling out, "Help! Oh, Star. Someone help!" Star was staring at her as if she couldn't believe what she was hearing. Apparently, there was a heart under Cora's newly formed breasts.

Before any of the men could get to the circle of kids watching the bloodbath, another young man called Willie out. He stood there in front of this tyrant from the swamp and said, "She's not *your* woman!"

Star slapped her hands over her eyes, but only after she had taken a good look at Lester Weeks. He was dressed in ice-cream trousers and a soft-looking shirt the color of buttermilk.

Willie laughed as Lester stuck out his jaw, seemingly in anticipation of a hard smack. Nathan stepped into the circle, too. A half dozen other boys followed his example. Alvin again tugged on Willie's arm, and they backed away.

Some of the girls knelt beside Wendall and patted his bleeding face with their handkerchiefs. Among them was Betty Weeks, looking as radiant as if she were offering her services to a dying man on the battlefield.

I looked at Nathan's face. He was no longer worried about Star. He had found Betty in the cluster and was looking her

71

over, from the emerald green ribbon in her hair to the soft arches of her leather shoes.

"You know I'm good for you, Shining Star," Willie said as he and Alvin disappeared into the woods.

Nathan and the other boys pulled Wendall to his feet. Wendall was smiling sheepishly at all the girls. Most of them hurried inside to carry the gossip to their mamas, but Cora, who I had expected to be the first to wag a tattling tongue, came over to stand beside Star and me.

Star said, "Thank you, cousin, for calling out for help for me."

Cora looked surprised. "I did?"

We nodded yes.

She turned to walk away, mumbling, "Imagine that."

7

Nathan came over Saturday morning to set up the dishwasher for Mama. Star and I sat at the kitchen table and watched the two of them fuss over the contraption that was made of brushes, a little motor, and a long cord that connected them.

Nannie had left very early with Mr. Avartoz to take Ezra to see the doctor, so Mama decided to place the regular breakfast dishes into the big tin sink before Nathan arrived. I tried to convince her to use old plates, but she thought that would be an insult to Nathan.

Nathan pumped water into the sink and said, "It's all ready."

Mama said, "Let 'er rip."

Nathan started the motor. It hummed like a bee in a hive for a moment, then sent its energy into the invention in the sink. Just as Nathan promised, the brushes on a spoked wheel began to spin. They churned the water, and everything seemed to be working.

The first sound that let us know all was not right was the high-pitched screech of glass breaking. That sound was followed by another and another just like it.

Nathan bolted toward the motor and turned it off. Mama reached into the churned water and pulled out a piece of plate. Even to the unscientific eye it was plain to see what had happened. All the little brushes on the spokes had come off

73

and upon closer inspection could be seen floating in the dishwater like tiny, capsized canoes.

"I used a real strong glue," Nathan breathed. "Didn't think the water would do it any harm."

Mama continued to pick out pieces of plate. Only one, on the bottom, was unscratched. She held it up and said, "We'll use this one as a platter."

"Sorry, Sarah," Nathan said softly. "I'll make it up to you."

Mama smiled weakly. "Nonsense. Name one of your inventions after me when you're successful. That would be plenty."

I could tell from Mama's expression that she was trying to think of something to tell Nannie. We all knew gadgets and notions were not Nannie's cup of tea.

Nathan nodded and retrieved his damaged machine from the sink. He left a trail of water on the kitchen floor as he lugged the dishwasher outside and placed it in the back of his daddy's truck. Star excused herself to her room, and I followed Nathan outside.

"Made a fool of myself on that one," he said to me.

"If you don't try, how will you ever know if anything works," I said, trying to comfort him.

"I just wanted to show you what I could do."

I didn't know what to say to Nathan. He was looking at me as if I was supposed to know *exactly* what to say.

Finally he said, "I expect you're going to win at that talent search your mama is taking you to."

My mind whirled. "What's the talent search have to do with all of this?" I blurted.

"You'll win. I just know it," Nathan said solemnly.

"So?"

"If you win, you and your mama will move away from Guthrie. I won't see you anymore."

"I would come back. I like it here. This is where I'm from."

"You'll go away and stay."

"Nathan, are you telling me if someone goes away and becomes successful at something they won't come back home?"

He got into the truck. "If you go too far away, if you learn too much, if you change, you won't be happy here. Why, your mama can hardly stay in town a day without jumping in her auto and heading out somewhere. Everyone knows how she's stirring up the dirt on the road. Everyone talks. She's got wandering fever or something —"

"People should mind their own business."

"And take your uncle Eli —"

"What about him?" I asked, surprised at the anger in my voice.

"He left. He went to France. When he got back he didn't give a hen's tooth about Guthrie." Nathan moved his arms back and forth like his daddy did when he was preaching. "You leave and you won't care about friends or family or . . . me."

"I am going to Little Rock," I said. "But just because I'm trying something new doesn't mean I dislike everything old. Like old friends and old feelings."

Nathan stammered a moment before he said, "Then there's Nan. Folks talk about how she's done so much for so many people, and her own children won't even stay around long enough to give her some help. Folks say she's working herself to death taking care of those old people. Working herself to death."

"Nannie has her life to lead. I suppose Eli and Mama and Star have all made mistakes, but Nannie always intended for them to have their own lives. Nannie says baby chicks have to leave the chicken yard and go out on their own."

"Fly the coop, huh?" Nathan asked with a lighter tone. He started the truck. "Be at church tomorrow? We have a guest evangelist."

"Nannie has planned for all of us to go. Your family and guest are invited for dinner."

Nathan softened his voice and asked, "Will you sit by me?"

I nodded that I would.

"See you then," Nathan said. He shut the truck door and drove away.

I watched him until he was past the lane. Then I turned to go inside. Mama met me at the back door. I could tell from her expression that she had heard it all. "Looks like 'folks' are talking again. Did Nan really say baby chicks have a right to leave the coop?"

"It makes sense," I said.

"The biggest problem, Laurie girl, is that the fence is so high," Mama said, tipping her head to the side as if she were a sage.

I loved Mama very much, but at that moment I wanted to make her feel a pang of guilt about the way she treated Nannie. To give her just a little twist of the heart, I said, "Someday I'll want to leave you, too, Mama."

Mama didn't flinch. She said instead, "'Spect you're old enough to know what you want."

"Yes, ma'am," I said as I pushed by her into the already hot kitchen.

That Sunday after church Nathan's family, the visiting evangelist, and Aunt Nola's family arrived to eat lunch.

After the meal Nannie said, "You girls do the dishes while we adults retire to the parlor."

I said, "Yes, ma'am," but Star glared at Nannie, apparently unhappy that Cora was included.

After the guests had followed Nannie and the others out of the kitchen, Cousin Cora began to carry the food bowls to the cabinet. I began to help, too, and Star sat down and folded her arms.

"I'll wash," I said. "Star, why don't you dry. Cora, you can put things away."

Star kicked back her chair and stood up. "I hate all this togetherness. I have important things to think about."

Cora asked, "What kinds of things?"

"Trust me, it's something you wouldn't understand," Star said.

"What things?" Cora persisted.

Star rolled her eyes. "I'm thinking about going away. About getting a job in Little Rock. Or maybe I'll go up to Joplin, Missouri. We have cousins there —"

"Guess I would understand," Cora said flatly.

Star mumbled, "You never thought about getting farther than your mama's apron strings in your life."

Cora took after her then, tea towel in hand, saying, "I have thought about it. I think about it every day. And I don't think about it *all by myself,* either!"

"Well, la-di-da," Star said, level with Cora's gaping teeth. "You have a secret. *Imagine that!*"

That was it. The end of conversation for over forty-five minutes. No matter what we said, Cora said nothing. She just walked like a marionette from the cabinet to the cupboard to put away the plates. When we were finished, she disappeared out the back door.

I had perked a fresh pot of coffee, and Star and I carried it with cups on a tray into the parlor. Aunt Nola was playing the piano as if her fingers were little hammers on an anvil. Nannie was cringing as she sang "Shall We Gather at the River" with the others.

Star and I served the coffee and were about to leave when Mama said, "Laurie, won't you sing for us?"

I wanted to say no, but Mama's eyes were pleading with

me, so I asked, "Aunt Nola, will you play 'Amazing Grace'?"

She nodded and began to play the old hymn with a softer touch.

I opened my mouth, and the song flowed out of me as easily as water along the banks of the Wigerstat, as easily as a butterfly through the mountain air. It was as if all of me was focused in that sweet, soft strand of music that was coming, almost mysteriously, out of me.

When I finished everyone clapped loudly. Aunt Nola raised her hands toward the ceiling and said, "I believe Laurie has a blessed voice."

I thought I had just done a particularly good job of staying on key.

"Laurie's going to enter the talent search over at Little Rock," Mama said quickly.

Nannie looked at me and smiled.

Aunt Nola glanced at the evangelist and then said to Mama, "Do you really think that is such a good idea? Taking a young girl to a talent search? She'll be wanting to sing on the stage, then, and one thing leads to another —"

Mama said hotly, "I imagine Laurie can sing about anywhere she chooses and please the Lord."

Aunt Nola looked at Mama and softened her voice as she said, "I expect that's so." She began to play another tune, and the others sang along.

Star turned on her heels and hurried out of the room. I ran after her, but she was beyond the back door by the time I caught up. Mama was following me. At the door, she put her hand on my shoulder.

"Don't pay attention to what any old woman says about singing outside the church," Mama said.

"Aunt Nola seemed surprised that I would even think of doing such a thing," I said.

"There's no bogeyman on the stage." Mama patted my arm. "And you can please the Lord by singing on the radio. I'm certain of it."

Mama moved me aside and stepped onto the porch. She called to Star, who was just beyond the barn, to wait up. Star stopped and waited while Mama walked to her. Then they went, arm in arm, across the meadow toward the swamp.

Cora came to stand beside me, and we watched them until they were out of sight.

"Wonder where the two of them are going?" Cora asked.

When I didn't answer, Cora got her shawl and hurried after them, not taking a direct route, but rather scurrying along the woods and proving herself to be the little weasel Star thought she was.

8

The next Tuesday afternoon was the monthly meeting of what the community had come to call the Widows Club. Four women attended: Nannie; Aunt Nola; Fannie Taylor, Wendall's mother; and Rhetta Harper. Their husbands had built a lumber mill in Guthrie in 1914. It had been the pride and joy of the community. Everyone had settled in to make a fortune.

In the fall of 1918, while Papa Gabriel and the other three men were working on a new headsaw, the side of the mill collapsed. All of them were crushed under piles of rubble.

All four men were buried in the little cemetery by the Baptist church. After their deaths, enthusiasm in the mill decreased. By the time the federal government opened up western timberlands, and the companies out there could ship their lumber east even cheaper than the folks of Guthrie could cut it, the lumber mill business had already collapsed. Depression hit Guthrie long before the stock market crashed in 1929.

Mama always suspected that the four widows kept Guthrie from being any more than a farming town. There was bitterness festering in all of them like an unlanced boil. To Mama's greatest sorrow, Nannie was their leader.

And their club was to have a guest that afternoon. It was to be Wally Weeks. We hadn't seen much of him since his family had moved to the river house. When we did see him he was usually standing around with a group of men, puffing on a big cigar and telling tales of the riches to come. Mr. Weeks had really invited himself to the meeting. The widows didn't like to share their grieving time with anyone.

Star and I served the ladies lemonade in the parlor. Then we sat in the hallway to be available if Nannie called for anything more. Star shooed the boarders to their rooms several times, but they kept leaking down the stairs to listen.

To Star's disgusted surprise Lester was with Mr. Weeks when he arrived and was carrying a bunch of lilacs big enough to pass as a funeral wreath. Lester held the flowers out to Star, and she attempted to ignore them. It was something like falling in the creek and pretending you didn't get wet.

"I'll put them in a vase," I said as I took the bouquet from Lester.

Lester coughed and went back to the porch.

"Well, you look as if you're going to a funeral, Wally," Nannie said as she looked Mr. Weeks over, from his starched collar to his high-topped boots.

"I dressed to impress," he said cheerily as he escorted her back into the parlor.

Star and I quickly dragged our chairs to where we could spy in the parlor door without being noticed.

"Let me get you some lemonade," Aunt Nola said. She got up, sauntered across the floor, and poured with a flourish.

Mrs. Taylor and Mrs. Harper scooted apart on the settee so Mr. Weeks could sit between them. Nannie and Aunt Nola pulled chairs close, and Nannie asked, "Now, Wally, what did you want to see us about?"

Mr. Weeks paused, looking into the faces of each of the women. "I heard the group of you are the heart and soul of this community."

The women tittered.

81

Mr. Weeks continued, "I heard your husbands were responsible for growth and prosperity in this community."

"That was a long time ago," Nannie said with an edge to her voice.

Mr. Weeks reached over and took Nannie's hand. "I know your husbands' deaths were difficult to face. I know —"

Nannie interrupted, "Wally, what is it you want? Money?"

Mr. Weeks straightened up. "Well, yes, money. I need some people from the community to invest in the shoe factory. You would be in on the ground level. You would be doing the community a great service —"

"We don't have any money to spare," Nannie said.

"This is a good business you have here," Mr. Weeks said, glancing around the room.

Nannie got up and walked over to stand behind Aunt Nola. "We've had about all the experience in business we needed with the lumber mill."

No one else said a word.

Finally, Mr. Weeks looked at the others and asked, "Does Nan speak for all of you?"

Aunt Nola said, "We're pretty much set in our ways."

"Yes, we are," Fannie Taylor agreed.

"And you, Mrs. Harper, what about you? Your husband started the mill. It was his idea. Mr. Roth told me all about it. Your husband was a man of vision. Do you think he would have wanted Guthrie to turn back to dust?" Mr. Weeks asked.

Mrs. Harper didn't answer.

"Guthrie isn't dust," Nannie said defensively.

"There's nothing to keep your young people here," Mr. Weeks said.

"I have no money to invest," Nannie said. She moved toward the door.

When the others didn't speak, Mr. Weeks got up and said, "Thank you for the lovely refreshments. Think about what I said, ladies. I'll get in touch again."

Nannie showed him out. It was all Star and I could do to move our chairs back fast enough so Nannie wouldn't see we had been listening. We would have made a clean getaway, but the boarders couldn't move that quickly and ended up half-way up the stairs, staring at Nannie like hounds with egg on their faces.

"Enjoy the show?" Nannie asked all of us as she returned to the parlor.

"What show?" Mama asked as she came in from the kitchen. When there was silence, Mama peeked into the parlor, asking, "What has the Old Widder's Club been up to?"

"Mr. Weeks came by and asked them to invest in the shoe factory," I told her.

"You're kidding!" Mama squealed. "He had the nerve to ask *them*? They haven't had an original thought concerning how to make a living since they picked up the hoe, pumped the sewing machine, and opened this boardinghouse."

"Those are all honorable ways to make a living," Apples said from her place on the stairs.

Mama didn't answer. She seemed to be somewhere else as she walked onto the porch.

"Mama's up to something," I told Star.

Later that evening Mama had me meet her on the front porch to rehearse the number I was taking to the talent search.

Mama sat down on the steps and began to strum chords on her dulcimer. "I thought you might sing 'Let a Smile Be Your Umbrella.'"

"Mama, I'm going to Little Rock. Isn't that song pretty much contemporary? What about singing a folk song from around here?"

"There will be big-time agents at the talent search. They won't want to hear hillbilly music. If you want to sing those kinds of songs, stay at the Community Building."

There was something taunting about her tone I didn't like.

Mama began to strum the dulcimer again. "Well, sing your song for me."

I belted out "Let a Smile" and tried to be animated.

Mama said, "If that's the way it's going to be we might as well not plan on making the trip."

"What's wrong?" I asked.

"Your heart isn't in it. That's one thing I'm a pretty good judge of, whether a performer has her heart in it."

"I like folk tunes."

"So you said."

"Look, Mama, I don't want to go to Little Rock and end up looking like a fake."

"You wouldn't look like a fake. You would look like someone who has a little more *culture* than the people around here."

"Are you ashamed of our people?" I asked.

Mama hesitated before she said, "No, I'm not ashamed. I don't intend for you to be ashamed. I just think you should sing something that would appeal to an audience other than the people who gather at the Community Building."

"I'll sing what you want me to sing," I said, seeing what I thought were tears in her eyes.

"That's fine. Now you keep practicing and plan to leave early Friday morning. That should give us plenty of time to get there," Mama said with the tone she used when she wanted to forget about something. "Oh, by the way, I have invited Star to come along with us."

"You have?" I asked. "Can Nannie get by without her?"

"Nan will have to get by without her," Mama said.

Every Thursday morning Nannie received her copy of the Sunday *Little Rock Globe* in the mail. It took that long for the delivery man to make the trip from Little Rock to the store at Crossroads. Nannie didn't mind waiting on the news, saying if it was news that really mattered to her she would know about it anyway. I suspected she ordered the paper just to get the sports scores, the only part of the paper, in her opinion, worth reading.

Nannie's "paper reading ritual" was another of her little quirks. The *Globe* was to be placed by her chair in the parlor, still in its brown wrapper, untouched, until she had time to read it in the afternoon before supper. After that, all of the paper was fair game to any other reader.

The Thursday before we were to leave for Little Rock, Nannie went into the parlor, glass of lemonade in hand, and had time to sit down before she let out a banshee cry, "Where is the *Globe*?"

"I didn't touch it!" Star yelled from the back porch.

I hurried to the parlor. "Nannie, I don't think anyone went to the store to pick it up," I said.

Nannie slapped her palm against her head. "I believe you're right. Your mama has been so excited about getting you to the talent search, she forgot the mail."

"I'll go to the store and get the paper for you," I volunteered.

"You wouldn't mind, honey?"

"I'll walk along the river. It won't take long."

I left Nannie to drink her lemonade and went out the back door.

Star was sitting on the porch. "Going to get the paper, I hear. I'll walk along with you if you'll buy me a soda."

I dashed back inside and got my coin purse.

We walked for a half mile without speaking. Finally I said, "Do you want to talk or something?"

Star stopped quickly and dug her toe in the dirt before she said, "Talk about what?"

"About us. About me entering the talent contest. About Mama. About Nathan. You name it."

Star looked up. "Remember when we first saw Betty Weeks and you said, 'God must love some people more than others'?"

"I remember."

"You know, I think He does. Lester was telling me that Betty really is as sweet and kind as she lets on. I don't think he would lie to me —"

"You've been seeing Lester?"

Star glared at me. "A couple of times, at the river."

"You sure didn't act very nice to him when he brought you flowers."

"He surprised me, that's all. I hate it when I'm surprised, especially in front of all those old people."

"They're interested in you, that's all," I said. "They enjoy your adventures. You always give them something to talk about."

"Yeah?"

"Star, they love you."

"It's easy for you to say those things because you get a chance every now and then to get away. I'm stuck here. Yeah, you're like Betty. You have it all. You're going to get what you want out of life."

86

"What do you think I want?"

"Out of here," Star said, scoffing.

"Away from Guthrie?"

"Who doesn't want away from Guthrie?"

"I don't."

Star laughed wickedly. "Then why are you going to Little Rock?"

"If I'm going to be a singer, I have to go," I said.

Star's face reddened. "And then you're out of here, like Sarah. Like Eli."

"I intend to come back."

"Only to visit."

I threw up my hands. "What do you want from me? Do you want me to stay home and marry Nathan? Do you want me to live with Nannie forever? What?"

"Nathan's a good catch, and I'm going to be with Nan forever. I don't have any talent. I'm not very pretty. And I'm not good in school. I'm going to marry some good old boy —"

"With gravy on his chin?"

"Yes, with gravy on his chin and be a regular slew-foot Sue and have a baby in the cradle and one on my hip and ten in the front yard chasing the chickens."

"No, you're not," I said. I had the greatest urge to take Star into my arms and hold her.

"I am and you know it." The words spurted out, and Star began to cry then, great shaking sobs like a man cries at his mama's funeral. Star stood there weeping for a moment before she stepped toward me and let me put my arms around her.

"You can do anything you want to do," I assured her, even though I wasn't certain it was a fair promise.

"Okay." She was still crying.

"I love you, Star."

87

She squeezed me and said, "I love you, too."

Then she stopped crying as quickly as she had started. "You tell anyone about this, and I'll make you eat mud."

I laughed. "Do you really want me not to go to Little Rock?"

"You have to go, don't you?" Star asked me as she took my arm and led me down the road to Crossroads Store.

I didn't answer, except to myself. And I knew that I did.

We picked up the *Globe* and, with the paper tucked under Star's arm and the grape Nehis in our hands, started back home. Where the river flowed through Little Deacon Highlands, Star sat down.

"Don't you think we'd better hurry back? Nannie will be champing at the bit for her paper," I said.

"I think I'll read it first," Star said with a hint of her old self. She gently pulled off the wrapper, which told me she didn't really want Nannie to know she had read the paper first, and scanned the front page.

I sat down beside her and watched the butterflies tease the flowers in the meadow. After a few minutes I asked, "Anything interesting?"

Star didn't answer.

I turned toward her. She was as white as a sun-dried sheet. "What's wrong?" I asked.

"There's a bonus army marching to Washington, D.C., this month," she whispered.

"I know. I heard about it on the radio. Veterans from the war are trying to get more rights. Said they would camp outside the capitol until the president did something for them," I said to Star, whose face had grown somber. "When did you get interested in politics?"

"When my brother became interested," Star said as she dropped the paper.

With a trembling hand I reached for the *Globe* and looked

long at the photograph on the front page. There, with much the same expression as he had in a picture Mama carried in her wallet, was Uncle Eli holding a sign that said WASHINGTON OR BUST.

I stood up quickly. "Let's hurry and show Nannie."

Star exploded. "No! She won't want to see him. Eli is as good as dead to her. She doesn't talk about him. She certainly wouldn't want to see a picture of him." She removed the front page from the paper, folded it, and put it in her dress pocket.

"Mama saw Uncle Eli at least once after the war," I said. "She told me about it. He was getting married and wanted her to meet his bride. They had dinner. Mama has always told me Eli had his reasons for leaving Guthrie, and that we shouldn't hold it against him."

"Eli just walked out," Star said. "He had the nerve to say no to Nan. I can understand it, but I've always hated him for it. Hated him for leaving me here with Nan and all those old, petrified people."

"I wish you'd stop feeling so sorry for yourself."

It was the wrong thing to say. Star jumped up and started walking, folding the rest of the paper as she left. "I'm going to find out," she bellowed.

"Find out what?" I asked as I hurried to catch up.

"Find out from Eli why he decided not to come home. He owes me that."

"Nannie will never let you see him."

"He's in Little Rock. Aren't we going to Little Rock? Without Nan? It's my only chance."

"You think Mama will let us see him?"

"Sarah can go with us. Sarah can stay away. I don't care what she does," Star said. She slapped the paper against her leg and walked away.

At the house Nannie looked at the paper and said, "What happened to it?"

I glanced at Star. She said, "Someone must have read it at the store. The cover was torn off and the front page was missing."

"Well, I'll declare, what will people be getting into next?" Nannie said hotly.

Star walked out of the room, saying over her shoulder, "I expect you'd think some news isn't worth reading."

It wasn't until late that night that I thought more about what Star had said to me. I felt guilty wanting more than what I could have in Guthrie. I should have been happy. I had a nice place to live, family who loved me, and Nathan. Maybe Uncle Eli had felt the same way. It wasn't that he hated Guthrie. He simply wanted something more.

I took a moonlight walk through the orchard. When I got back to the house, Nannie met me on the back porch. "I saw you leave and began to think you had gotten lost or something," she said, slipping her arm around me.

"I was thinking," I said.

"About what?" Nannie pulled her wrap around her shoulders.

"About this place. About you and Mama and Star and . . ."

"And Eli?"

"I don't think I remember ever hearing you say his name. How'd you know I was thinking about him?" I asked.

"You're thinking about leaving. Eli always comes to mind when a person is thinking about leaving."

I moved away from Nannie so I could look at her face. "You don't want me to go to Little Rock, do you?"

"You like the farm."

"That's right."

"I thought you might be the one who wanted it," Nannie said.

"I still might be the one."

"But you want other things too?"

90

I took Nannie's hands into mine. "I think I do. I would never have figured it out without Mama pushing me into it, but I really think I would like to sing. Every time I think about it, I get goose bumps."

"I get goose bumps when I garden," Nannie said.

"Tomatoes never had that effect on me."

Nannie smiled. "I get goose bumps when I'm helping people."

"Do you think some people go through life without ever feeling that strongly about anything?" I asked.

"I'd say most people go through life just that way," Nannie said, mostly to herself.

"It's all right with you if I go? I won't go if you want me to stay."

Nannie leaned against a post. "Sing for me, Laurie."

"Right now?"

"Right here and now."

"It's late. The boarders will throw shoes."

Nannie laughed softly. "I don't think so. They all sleep like stones."

"A request?"

"A love song. One about a broken heart."

"Broken hearts are my specialty," I said. Then I sang an old, sad tune. When I finished, Nannie didn't say anything. She gave me a quick hug before she went inside.

I was left alone with the night: the crickets and tree frogs chirping, the moon playing hide-and-seek behind the clouds, and the sweet scent of peaches ripening. I had started inside when I heard a window screen open.

"That was mighty pretty singing, Laurie," Apples said from her upstairs room.

"Mighty pretty," several others chorused.

"The gang's all here," I said. "God bless the gang."

91

9

Mama, Star, and I arrived in Parnell, Arkansas, at Nannie's cousin Eloise's house about midnight Friday. Eloise woke us up at six o'clock the next morning so we could get to Little Rock before the talent search at two o'clock that afternoon. We were on the road by seven o'clock, and our spirits were high, maybe because of the excitement but probably because of feeling so free of responsibility.

"This is the life," Star said as she laid her head against the front seat.

Mama glanced her way and smiled. "A rolling stone gathers no moss."

"I could be a rolling stone," Star said quickly.

I said, "Nannie would say you should be a stone in a fence. A nice, strong fence built with others in your family. There is nothing more important in this world than *family*."

"You should lecture me," Star said, sitting up. "You're rolling about as far and fast as you can."

Mama started to say something, but cut off her own words and drove with a vengeance.

We crossed the Arkansas River from North Little Rock into Little Rock just before noon. We didn't have time to find a hotel before the talent search, so we went to a café, and I used the sink and mirror in the toilet to freshen up. I felt pretty calm about the whole thing, but Mama was a mess.

She paced as if she were a daddy expecting triplets and

constantly hurried everyone along. That didn't settle very well with Star, who was leisurely enjoying every moment of her newfound freedom.

"We'll be late," Mama said as she herded us back into the auto. "The man at the café told me how to get to Broadway Avenue."

She steered the Packard down a side street. After about fifteen minutes of driving she pulled up in front of a tall, red brick building surrounded by a jungle of holly trees.

"Is this the place?" Star asked as she peered out.

The fact that the building was about ten stories tall seemed to be what attracted Star's attention. I was looking at the long line of people standing on the sidewalk and stretching around the building like a lumpy snake.

"Looks as if everyone from every little hill and hollow has come to perform," I said to Mama.

All she said was, "Tune your guitar."

I got out, retrieved my guitar from the little storage space behind the back seat, and leaned against the bumper to tune it.

"Remember to smile," Mama said.

"Okay."

"Say all your words clearly," she continued.

"Okay."

Mama asked Star, "What time is it?"

Star looked at the old watch Nannie had let her wear. She said dramatically, "Ten minutes before Laurie was *supposed* to sing."

Mama pulled a crumpled envelope from her handbag. She took a letter out of it, read it slowly to herself, and said, "Your session is at two o'clock."

"Are all these other people in line before me?" I asked.

"Let's go inside and find out," Mama said.

Star stayed behind, leaning on the automobile and smiling at a young man who was holding a fiddle, wrapped in a blanket, as if it were his firstborn child.

Mama and I were greeted inside by a tired-looking secretary with three pencils tucked over her right ear.

"You have an appointment, or should I give you a number?" the secretary asked. When she spoke, the pencils moved up and down.

"We have an appointment for Laurie Hargrove at two o'clock," Mama answered.

The secretary looked over a long paper, shook her head, turned the page, and said, "So you do."

"Well?" Mama asked.

"Well, take a seat," the secretary said with a tone of annoyance.

Mama guided me toward a bench near the door, then she turned to the secretary and asked, "Who are those people outside? Do they have appointments?"

The secretary glanced toward the window. "Most of those people didn't hear about the talent search until a few days ago. Others didn't have the money to mail back the entry form. They'll all get their chance, though."

Mama looked bewildered.

"Don't worry, it shouldn't cause you any grief," the secretary said flatly. "Except that you'll have to wait until they have all performed before we announce the winners."

"When would that be?" Mama asked.

"Late this evening. Maybe morning," the secretary said.

Mama sat down beside me. "Remember —"

"Smile. Say my words clearly," I answered.

Before Mama could say anything more, a heavy door slid open and a man in a brown pin-striped suit said, "Laurie Hargrove, please."

I stood up and walked toward the man. I swear, I could feel Mama's spirit walking beside me.

Inside the audition room were three other men, all in suits, and a woman with black hair done up in ringlets. The woman had a plain, happy face and a smile that would brighten a wake.

"What you gonna sing, honey?" the woman asked as she reached out for the music I had in my hand.

"It's a new tune," I said. "I heard it when I was in New York."

"You've been to New York?" one of the men asked me.

"I lived there for two years," I said, smiling.

He didn't smile back. He merely poised his pencil over a long yellow pad and seemed to be waiting for me to begin.

The woman looked over the music, passed it to the men, and asked, "You fellows ready?"

They nodded like crows on a clothesline, and the woman said, "Hit a few licks, honey, and then let it rip."

I strummed my guitar and sang. To me it sounded as if I were gargling under water. I began to figure that it sounded that way to them too because they were already writing on their pads and not even looking at me while I performed. My insides felt wobbly, and there was something in the back of my throat that tasted like cottage cheese. I finished the song and left the sound of a hollow guitar echoing in the room.

The woman said, "Thank you, honey. The results will be posted on the bulletin board out front, hopefully sometime today. If not, check in the morning."

I somehow managed to move and let myself out the door.

Mama stood up the moment she saw me. She looped her arm through mine and led me outside, whispering, "How did you do?"

"They didn't like me," I managed to say.

Star walked toward us, asking, "Did you forget the words or something?"

"They didn't like me," I repeated.

"Let's forget about your performance for now. We'll know how you did soon enough," Mama said with a distinct touch of Nannie in her voice.

It was all a blur after that. We got in the Packard, and Mama drove to the Barker Hotel. We got a room on the second floor. It had a little balcony and an inside toilet.

We had lunch sent up from the café downstairs and ate it as we rested. I kept waiting for Star to ask Mama if she would take us to see Uncle Eli. I thought she was going to do it a couple of times, but she always ended up putting a bite of sandwich in her mouth and chewing it until it was vapor.

When we were finished Mama said, "Well, you girls stick around here. I told Nan I'd do some shopping for her. We'll get sodas when I get back."

Star almost said something, but she didn't, and we watched Mama leave.

"Why didn't you ask her?" I asked Star.

"She would have said no. I felt it in my bones," Star said with her sage voice.

"Now what?"

"We'll find Eli on our own."

"I'm not sure that's such a good idea," I said.

Star began to brush her hair. "If you can look me right in the eyes and tell me you don't want to see him at all, we'll call this whole thing off."

"I'll give it a shot," I said. "Come over here so I can get a good look."

Star put down her hairbrush and walked over to me. She looked into my eyes. "You're getting taller."

"You're shrinking."

Star smiled.

96

I wanted to tell her I didn't want to see Uncle Eli, but the look I saw deep within her nearly shook me to my roots. It was a look of pain and curiosity — and love. "You've got me. I can't say seeing Eli doesn't matter."

"Then we've got some detective work to do," Star said, opening the hotel room door.

I thought being on the trail of Uncle Eli would be like a chapter in a dime novel, but finding him was so simple, it took all the fun out of it. Star merely went to a phone book in the lobby of the hotel and looked up Gabriel. There in plain English was a listing for Eli Thomas Gabriel, 205 Elm Street.

"Where is Elm Street?" Star asked the man at the front desk.

"Two streets over, right near where Capitol picks up Broadway," he said.

"And where would 205 be on the street?" Star asked.

"Two blocks down," the man answered.

"We could holler, and Eli would hear us," I said to Star.

"Eli?" the man asked. "Eli Gabriel?"

Star looked as if she had been slapped. "You know him?"

"Delivers ice here every afternoon," the man said. "Fine businessman."

"Would he be at home now?" I asked.

"We're his last delivery, so if he isn't helping out at the fire department or over at the church, he'll be home," the man said.

Star said, "Thank you," and hurried out the door. When I caught up with her, she said, "Eli is just a regular little old pillar in the community, isn't he?"

"We're interfering with his life," I said.

Star picked up her pace. "He has certainly interfered with ours, don't you think?"

We were still arguing when 205 Elm Street loomed before

us. It was a nice, big house with a well-kept lawn full of ceramic figurines and flowers. An ice truck with Gabriel Ice Company lettered in red on its side was parked in the driveway. There was a crisp, white wash on the clothesline in back and three small children chasing a puppy across the front yard.

"Home, sweet home," Star said. She boldly walked to the front door and rang the chime.

I stood near the brick sidewalk and wished I was anywhere but there.

A dark-haired powder puff of a woman answered the door with a soft, "Yes, may I help you?"

"I would like to speak with Eli Thomas Gabriel," Star said firmly.

I smiled at the woman.

"Who may I say is calling?" the woman asked.

"Are you Eli's wife?" Star blurted.

"Yes, I'm Gretchen," the woman said with a puzzled tone.

Before Star could say anything more, a hand pulled open the door farther, and Uncle Eli stepped onto the porch. He looked long at Star and then at me.

"So you found me," he said to us. His tone was almost one of amusement. Star stood, speechless, looking into Uncle Eli's face.

"Come with me," he said as he moved down a hall and pushed open a door. We followed him. I was feeling sick at my stomach.

As we walked into Uncle Eli's parlor, we saw Mama sitting on the sofa. She said, "I wondered if the two of you were up to something."

Star bellowed, "I don't much like finding you here, Sarah. Coming here without us is about as low as you can get."

Mama got up quickly. "Did either of you ask to see Eli? Well?"

"No, ma'am," I said.

"Star? Did you ask me?" Mama asked.

Star looked at her feet. "I guess not."

"I guess not," Mama said. She smiled at Eli. "Now, let's start this reunion over."

"You left us," Star gushed at Eli. She sobbed deep in her chest.

"Nannie has worried about you," I added.

Uncle Eli smiled kindly. "That's not quite the truth, is it? Nan is still angry."

"She'll go to her grave angry if you don't do something about it," Star said with tears running down her cheeks. "Just tell me why you didn't stay. With Papa dead, we needed a man to help out."

"There was nothing for me in Guthrie," Uncle Eli said. "Look, there was Nan and all those old people she likes to collect and Sarah with a new baby and you still in didies. I knew all that responsibility would have fallen on my shoulders. I was only a kid. I wanted a life of my own. I wanted to do some things. See some places. Go my own way."

"You could still have visited us," I said.

"I wanted to make a clean break," Eli said.

Mama had stood silent for the moments it took Star and me to have our say, then she turned toward Eli and said, "I do think it's about time you came home."

"Isn't that being a little hypocritical, Sarah?" Uncle Eli asked.

"I go home. I visit," Mama said.

"Nan still sets a place for you at the table," Star said, sobbing.

"Come home, Eli," Mama said.

Uncle Eli smiled. "Does Nan still put the ugliest scarecrow in the county in her garden?"

"Believe it or not, it's wearing a suit this year," Mama said.

99

Star continued to cry.

"Oh, Sarah," Uncle Eli said, the smile gone from his face. "It would be so hard to go back."

"I want to walk until I fall off the edge of the world," Star said to me as we stumbled along the sidewalk outside Uncle Eli's house.

"We saw him," I said.

"I bawled like a baby." Star kicked a rock in the road.

"Did you want him to repent?"

"Yes. I wanted him to beg for forgiveness."

"Maybe you are kin to Aunt Nola."

"Don't start," Star warned.

We walked for a while longer. "Want to go back to the hotel and order supper? Mama said she'd be along in a little while," I said.

Star shook her head. "I told you I want to walk until I fall off the edge of the world."

"You want an easy way out."

"I want a different life. I want Eli to come home, and I don't even want to stay at home. Nothing ever works out for me. The gods are against me."

"You mean God," I corrected.

She shook her head. "The gods. The Greeks and Romans had it right. There are a bunch of big wheels up in the sky moving us around like checkers on a board, giving us a break, making us squeal, for their own amusement."

"You're the silliest thing."

"One of them has his big, fat finger on my checker right now."

Luck. Maybe there was something to it. Maybe there were these "big wheels" in Heaven pushing us around. I lay on my bed at the hotel and thought about it for the longest time before Mama returned.

"Let's go see if the results of the talent search are posted," Mama said without even taking off her hat. She didn't even mention Uncle Eli.

Star was sitting on the balcony. She said, "I'll pass."

Mama shrugged and pointed toward the door. The trip to the red brick building on Broadway Avenue was a pilgrimage. Mama and I didn't talk to each other. We looked straight ahead. Only after she had parked her automobile did she say softly, "If you didn't do well, remember, this isn't the last door that will open for you."

I tried to speak, but nothing came out except that awful taste of cottage cheese.

On the bulletin board at the front of the building was a long piece of paper flapping in a light breeze. There were a few people gathered around it, pointing to this and that. The only one I remembered seeing before was the young man with the fiddle. He was smiling.

As we walked toward the list the young man said, "Got me a prize. Got me fifty dollars. Going to play on the radio."

"That's nice," Mama said as she pushed by him.

I stood back. Mama read the list. She read the list twice. Then a third time. She took me by the hand and led me inside where two of the men and the tired-looking secretary were stuffing papers into suitcases.

The man who hadn't smiled at me when I mentioned New York walked toward us. He pointed a finger in my face and said, "Stick to your own type songs, sweet face, and maybe you'll go somewhere."

"You didn't like the song Laurie sang?" Mama asked quickly.

The man raised his eyebrows. "Stick to your roots." He slammed his suitcase shut and hurried outside.

My ears burned. My teeth chattered. My stomach dived. Mama led me back to the automobile. "You were right," she

101

said. "You told me you wanted to sing something you had learned in Guthrie. I didn't listen. You could have won, maybe you could have. A kid with a piebald face and a fiddle that survived the Civil War beat you. He's going to be on the radio, and you're going to be listening to it, thanks to me."

I was so disappointed I couldn't think of a thing to say to comfort Mama. She put me in the auto, got in herself, and drove us back to the hotel. Star met us on the stairs. She didn't have to ask what had happened. I knew my jaw was hanging somewhere around my ankles.

"Sorry if my bad luck rubbed off on you," Star offered.

"There's no such thing as luck," Mama said. "There's talent and hard work and having the right idea at the right time."

I started to cry. I hated it when I did that. When I just stood like an idiot and sprang leaks.

Mama put her arm around me and said, "If it would make you feel any better you can take me to the woodshed."

"It wasn't your fault, Mama," I said.

"Yes it was. I was wrong. I have been wrong once or twice in my life." Mama smiled.

Star looked at Mama and me for a long time before she excused herself and went outside and stood under the gaslight.

10

We spent the night at the hotel and stayed until almost noon the next day. It was a mistake to have waited so late to start home because about two hours down the road we ran into a thunderstorm that had caused the highway to turn into a mud slide.

After fighting the weather until nearly dark, Mama pulled into a general store and asked if there was a place we could spend the night. When she came back to the auto to tell Star and me about it, she looked weary and was slow to speak.

"Well? Is there a place to sleep or not?" Star asked.

Mama said, "You won't like it."

"Why not?" I asked. "We're dead tired and wet and cold."

"It's a boardinghouse," Mama said flatly. She started the auto and steered it down a gravel road behind the general store.

Star didn't speak, but I knew she was believing she was cursed.

Mama found the boardinghouse after a couple of wrong turns. It was situated at the end of a long street and surrounded by a ring of trees that looked as if they belonged in a Halloween tale.

As we got out, Star said, "If they serve bat's wings, I'm leaving."

Mama mumbled, "I'll beat you to the Packard."

We followed Mama to the front porch and stood there for

103

a long time while she pounded on the door. Finally, a single bulb was turned on inside and an ashen-faced man opened the door and asked, "What you folks be a wantin'?"

"Do you have a room we could rent for the night?" Mama asked.

It was a question we had all heard asked at our front door a thousand times. And every time Nannie had opened the door wide and said, "Sure, we have a place for weary travelers. Come on in. Make yourselves at home."

But this old man looked us over from head to toe. I knew we looked like three drowned rats.

"Where you folks from?" he asked.

"Guthrie," Mama said.

"Three females away from home in the middle of the night," he said.

"We were visiting in Little Rock. We got caught in the storm," Mama said.

Star blurted out, "Look, mister, we're freezing. Are you going to let us rent a room or not?"

"You'd be expecting a meal, too, I reckon," he said.

"That would be nice," I said, trying to sound exceptionally sweet to cover up for Star's rudeness.

He opened the door wide and said, "Come on in."

It was past suppertime, but the table in the dining room was surrounded by old people slurping soup.

"We don't mean to impose," Mama said, glancing around.

It was plain to see that there was little food on the table. A piece of cooked cabbage was left with a small slice of boiled beef laying beside it. Some hard bread rounded out the meal.

"We'll just take sandwiches," Mama said.

The man nodded and walked to an open door. He called into the next room, "Evelyn, fix three sandwiches."

A frail voice said, "I'm a doin' it, Fred. I'm a doin' it."

The man turned toward us and said, "I'll get you some clean sheets."

After he was gone we were able to take a better look at the boarders. They were all as old as Methuselah, and they looked as if they didn't ever get to sit in the sunshine or drink fresh cider or smell lilac bouquets.

The man returned, gave Mama the sheets, got a tray of food from the kitchen, and led us up the stairs to a room that smelled like a cellar.

"How much do we owe you?" Mama asked.

"A dollar apiece. You can pay when you leave," he said.

"We may leave early. Here's your money," Mama said as she pressed the cash into his hand.

The man turned and went back down the stairs.

Mama switched on the single light hanging in the middle of the room and looked around the place. "Home, sweet home," she whispered as she set down the food tray.

We choked down the sandwiches, made the bed, and stripped to our underwear.

"I don't want to sleep in the middle," I said. "If there's reason to leave, I want a clear leap at the door."

"I'm not sleeping in the middle, either," Star said.

Mama sighed. "I'll sleep in the middle." She jumped on the bed and it sank. Star and I glanced at each other. I flicked off the light, and we piled in beside Mama. The mattress went nearly to the floor, apparently supported only by a dozen or so weak springs.

"Don't move. The bed will break," Mama breathed.

I turned against Mama and felt myself slipping into deep sleep. It was later, when my back began to hurt and I rolled over, that I heard Mama and Star talking.

Star said, "Are we going to tell Nan we saw Eli?"

Mama didn't answer at first. Then she said softly, "I think

we should wait until the time is right. Maybe after this factory thing is settled."

"Would it surprise you, Sarah, if I told you I felt bad seeing him behind Nan's back?" Star asked.

"You're not as tough as you pretend to be," Mama said.

There was a long moment of silence, and I almost went back to sleep, but Mama said in a louder voice, "What do you think of this boardinghouse?"

Star said, "It's a dump. Someone ought to turn it in to the county. It's dirty, and all those old people look sick and addled, to say the least. Nan wouldn't stand for any of it, not a bit. We have the cleanest, happiest boarders in the state."

"Don't we," Mama added.

I could practically hear the gears in Star's mind whirring. She had bragged on Nannie, and she wasn't quite sure what to make of it.

"I guess the difference is that Nan loves her old people," Star said as an afterthought.

"I guess that is the difference," Mama said.

I felt my heart swell and wanted to say something to both of them.

Mama put her arms around Star and me. Neither of them said anything more, but I knew from the breathing that all of us stayed awake and thought for a long time. We didn't move until the chickens crowed, and we dressed and slipped away.

Back at the farm there was no burial over my lost opportunity. Nannie said there would be a next time. I suspected that Aunt Nola secretly praised the Lord for not allowing me to go down the street of evil. Nathan smiled; I caught him. Mama was the only one who still made plans for me. She told me that after the Fourth of July she would tell me what they were. Then she left for Joplin, Missouri, to visit friends for the week.

The rest of us planned to celebrate the holiday the way we had for as long as I remembered. We would pack a picnic lunch, including a freezer of ice cream, and drive into town for the speeches and fireworks.

When I came down to breakfast on Independence Day I saw that Nannie had been awake for a long time. Most of the chicken was already fried. The pies were lined up, wearing wax paper tops to keep them fresh.

"Are we riding into town with Mr. Avartoz?" I asked.

"I'm not going into town today," Nannie said.

Star walked to the screen door. "What's that you say? You're not going?"

Nannie shook her head.

"Why not?" I asked.

"Ezra is sick. I'm going to stay home with him," Nannie said.

"Trust those old bones of his to give out on a holiday," Star said hotly.

"Those 'old bones' helped preserve the freedom we're celebrating today. Ezra fought in the War Between the States. He was a hero. He should at least have someone feed him a nice meal and sit with him on the front porch."

Later, after the rest of us were loaded into Mr. Avartoz's "beloved automobile," Nannie stood on the back porch waving good-bye.

As Mr. Avartoz turned toward town I said, "Stop, please."

Star said, "What are you doing?"

"I'm staying with Nannie," I said.

"You're trying to make me feel guilty for not staying and helping her," Star said softly.

"No I'm not," I said.

Mrs. Turner said from the back seat, "You'll miss all the pretty fireworks."

"Maybe I can come in before then," I said. I motioned for Star to let me out.

Star slid aside, and I hurried to the porch. As they drove away, I said to Nannie, "Thought you might need a little help with Ezra." Nannie put her arm around me, and we went in to have a glass of lemonade.

Later that afternoon, after Ezra had picnicked and drunk his fill of lemonade and waved his flag and settled down to nap, Nannie and I walked across the meadow to the graveyard beside the Baptist church. There weren't any ceremonies there this year. A lot of people said they didn't want to walk through the woods and stand around while some preacher droned on about the war dead.

"It's a sign of the times," Nannie said as she bent down and snagged the weeds around the first headstone she came to.

"What is?" I asked.

"When people choose not to honor those men who died for them, more men are going to die."

"You sound like Star believing those old wives' tales."

Nannie moved to another stone. "I have an excuse Star can't use. I *am* an old wife."

I kneeled beside her and helped her weed. "It doesn't seem right. All these young men killed in the prime of their lives."

"Man was born to die. Must be a greater honor to die for a cause, like freedom, than to one day fall behind your mule while plowing a rocky field."

We worked quietly until we came to my daddy's stone. It was tucked in beside Papa Gabriel's grave.

Nannie slipped her arm around me. "Do you ever think about your daddy?"

108

"Some. Probably not as much as you think about Papa Gabriel. I don't have the memories you have," I said.

Nannie sighed. "I've been thinking more and more about Papa since all this factory business started. You know, he would have been keen on putting it in."

"Mama says you're set in your ways, you and the —"

"Old Widder's Club?" Nannie finished.

"I don't think Mama means anything by it."

Nannie began to pull the dandelions from around Papa Gabriel's headstone. "There may be something to what your mama thinks."

"Mama said she'd been wrong once or twice."

Nannie continued to pull weeds. "Haven't we all."

"I think I'll pick some primrose on the ridge and put them here," I said.

Nannie nodded. When I brought the flowers back, she and I stood in the quiet graveyard for a while. I said a prayer for Daddy and Papa Gabriel. Nannie stood staring beyond the ridge of pines as if she were searching for someone. I thought how great it would be if Uncle Eli came walking over the hill, calling out for her. Nannie at least had the hope of seeing her son on this earth again. Hope was more than the mothers of all the other soldiers had.

11

That next Sunday while everyone was gathered around the dining table for the dinner of the "locusts," Mama came back from Joplin. You could say she came back with a "bang," because that's exactly what she did. She came back with a bang and a pop and a sizzle and a very, very old pickup truck.

After she had convinced the truck to remain parked, she opened its creaky door and came up onto the porch where Nannie, Star, and I waited for her.

"Dare I ask where your Packard disappeared to?" Nannie said softly.

Mama smiled and put her arms around Nannie. "I sold it."

"Why did you do that?" Star asked quickly as if her last means of escape had been disposed of.

"Why, Mama?" I asked, knowing that the Packard was Mama's prize possession.

"Having a big car didn't seem important anymore," Mama said wistfully. She herded us back into the house, smiled at Aunt Nola when she met her in the hall, and helped Nannie serve cake.

Nannie poured us coffee and sat down at the table beside Mama. "What's going on, Sarah?" she asked.

Mama took a long drink before she said, "We could all use the money that was tied up in that automobile for other things."

"What other things?" I asked.

110

"Ezra needs a wheelchair," Mama said.

Star looked confused.

"Nan, you could use a new wringer washing machine," Mama continued.

No one said anything.

"I intend to invest some money in the shoe factory," Mama said with the same matter-of-fact tone she had used for the other two revelations.

Nannie looked long at Mama before she said, "You're going to invest in — Guthrie?"

"Quite a switch, isn't it?" Mama said.

"I don't understand," I said. "You've always wanted to leave."

"There is also money to get you started on that singing career you have such talent for," Mama said to me. "I have even arranged an audition for you with Mr. Houser of WSB in Atlanta. I met him while I was in Joplin. He's very interested in hearing you sing."

Star looked as if she were going to come apart at the seams. "Isn't this a fine how-do-you-do, sister dear? All you have done for years is tell me how wonderful it is out in the big world and now you're suddenly perfectly happy to be the generous one, feathering your little nest. Why? What penance are you paying? Is it because you feel guilty about slipping around behind Nan's back all these years and seeing Eli?"

If a truckload of bricks had been dumped on the dining room table it wouldn't have had as much of an effect as the last line Star had blurted out. Star slapped her hand over her mouth and looked as if she wished a truckload of bricks would hide her.

"You've seen Eli?" Nannie asked flatly.

Mama said, "Yes."

"When you went to the talent search?"

111

"Then and other times," Mama said.

"We wanted to see him," I said.

Nannie nodded.

"We wanted to see him," Star whispered.

Nannie looked long at Star, then turned to Mama. "Sarah, do you have any idea how much this hurts me?"

"Yes, ma'am," Mama said with the voice of a little girl.

"And yet you did it?"

"It's time to let bygones be bygones," Mama said. "It's time to change —"

"Oh, now I get it. You think if you prove to me that you can change — for instance, get rid of that flashy automobile and put your money behind some factory jobs — then surely I can change, too, and welcome Eli home. Is that what you thought, Sarah?"

I spoke before I thought, "Those aren't nice things to say."

"So even you're turning against me, Laurie?" Nannie asked softly.

"I love you, Nannie. I'm not turning against you. It's just that I want us all to be together again," I said.

"I'm sorry I said anything," Star breathed, her cheeks scarlet. She got up and bolted for the back door.

Mama hurried after her. I stepped onto the porch and watched the chase across the meadow. Mama caught up with Star beside the orchard fence and managed to slow her down enough to talk to her.

I went back inside and sat down beside Nannie. We just sat there looking at each other and not speaking until we were startled by a loud pounding. It was Fannie Taylor, Wendall's mother, at the door.

Nannie jumped up and let Mrs. Taylor in. "Fix us some cool water, if you please, Laurie," Nannie said as she spirited her guest into a chair.

Mrs. Taylor's face was glowing. "I'm giving a little party Thursday evenin'. Wendall doesn't have much of a social life, and it seems to me that when he does get out, well, there's one kind of trouble or another."

Nannie said, "Star appreciated Wendall's help at the singing when Willie Tate was giving her a bad time."

"Then you will let Star and Laurie come, won't you? Wendall is so taken with both of them, and, of course, with Cora, too."

"Well, I should ask them —" Nannie started.

Mrs. Taylor interrupted. "They don't have to stay real late. Maybe nine o'clock or so. Enough time to have some fun. I haven't had a play party for Wendall since his sixth birthday, and he is so looking forward to this." She was breathless when she finished.

Nannie flashed a desperate look at me. I didn't speak.

Mrs. Taylor said, "We'll have iced drinks. I'm getting the block of ice in the morning and keeping it at my springhouse. And I'm making *apfel kissen* like my grandmamma made in Denmark. And there will be games, kissing games, and prizes, and —"

"That's very exciting," Nannie said, looking as if she felt she must stop Mrs. Taylor before she blew so much steam she collapsed.

"Then the girls will come?" Mrs. Taylor asked, smiling.

"They'll be there," Nannie conceded.

Mrs. Taylor smiled and stood up to leave. She patted me on the arm before she slipped out the back door.

Star came home around four o'clock that afternoon. She came into the kitchen with the wisps of hair around her face wet, which told us she had stopped at the well and washed away tears. Nannie poured her a glass of cider and set it on the kitchen table.

113

"I have something to say," Star said.

Nannie said, "Speak your piece."

"I'm sorry I told about Eli the way I did. I didn't mean to hurt you. I'm sorry I sneaked around to see him."

"It's all right," Nannie said. But she didn't make any movement that would have told Star to come hug her. Instead, she went out to sit on the front porch with Mr. Avartoz.

"Nannie will get over it," I said.

"I feel like a traitor."

"It wasn't wrong to see Eli. I believe Nannie knows we needed to see him."

"That's news to me," Star said.

"There is some news," I said to Star.

"What's that?" she asked softly.

"We've been invited to a party at Wendall's Thursday night."

"Who else is going?"

"I imagine every young person in the county has been invited."

"Will there be dancing?" Star asked.

"Only games, I figure. Nannie said Mrs. Taylor's daddy was a preacher, and although he didn't point a finger at all the vices, dancing was a sin of Sodom in his opinion. There will be *kissing* games."

"Then every big-lipped Benny this side of the Wigerstat will be there," Star said. "I'd better ask Lester to go, if he hasn't already been invited."

"Lester?" I asked, hardly believing what I heard.

"Lester's going to be someone important, I just know it," Star said.

Suddenly, Lester had gone from the beast to the acquaintance to Star's ticket out of Guthrie. "Does Lester know that

114

you've chosen him to escort you around the world?" I asked.

Star's mouth opened quickly and shut again and opened a second time, but no noise came out.

"You were going to say something?" I asked.

"Lester looks like a traveling man," Star said, mostly to herself.

"I wouldn't count on Lester or any other boy to make a life for you. You're perfectly capable of planning your future. Nannie has done a fine job as a businesswoman. Mama has a career."

"They're both still in Guthrie," Star said suddenly as she hurried upstairs.

I sat down on the back steps and thought about the changes in Mama. I sat there until Nannie came into the kitchen and began to fix supper. She was humming. It wasn't one of the old tunes she loved. It was something new off the radio. I suspected she didn't even know she was humming it, until she came to the door and said, "That's a new song by Maybelle Carter. You sing as good as she does, Laurie girl."

Maybe Nannie wanted to let me know she was really trying to catch hold of all the new things. At the same time I felt as if I were trying to hold on to all the old things. And Mama, she was stomping around somewhere out in the woods caught between the old ways and the new ways, trying to figure out which world wanted her.

I wore my pink "tooth fairy" dress to Wendall's party. Star wore a navy piqué with white polka dots on it. We stopped in the lane on the way there so Star could put on some rouge and lipstick.

"Want a little color?" she asked as she pushed the lipstick toward me. It was called Flaming Flamingo and was as pink as a bunny's ear.

"No, thanks," I said.

"Suit yourself," Star said as she crammed the lipstick into her handbag.

Star insisted we leave a half hour early and walked leaning forward as if that would get her there sooner. When I saw Lester waiting for her at the Taylors' front gate, it was all I could do to keep my mouth shut.

Lester was dressed in a pale blue suit. He had a bouquet of primroses in his hands and was grinning like an undertaker at a nursing home.

Star smiled at Lester, gave me a look that said, "If you say one word, it will be your last," and let him escort her to the Taylors' front porch.

I stood in the yard awhile until Nathan came out to the porch and asked, "Aren't you coming in?"

Wendall was beside him, his eyes sparkling with joy. "On my way," I said as I moved toward Nathan's outstretched hand.

Inside that little house were at least twenty people. All the furniture had been pushed against the walls and that helped some, but space was at a premium. Nathan and I stood wedged between the parlor and the dining room.

"This might be even more fun than I thought," Nathan said as he pressed against my side.

I looked into his eyes and saw questions. He must have realized that I noticed because he called out, "Where are all those games you promised, Wendall?"

Wendall said, "Mama, we're ready."

"Let the fun begin," Mrs. Taylor said.

We sang, we played charades, we ate apple turnovers and drank cider and chewed gum, and then Wendall got out the colored stick candy for the kissing game.

This wasn't candy to eat; this was candy to humiliate yourself with. Into a hat went the broken pieces of candy.

Twenty-four pieces in all. Twelve different colors. Everyone was to reach into the hat and retrieve a piece of candy. If two girls or two boys matched, they shook hands; but if the stick matched someone of the opposite gender, you had to kiss him on the lips or risk crowd discipline.

I suddenly wanted to go home, especially when my first match was with Wendall. You would have thought it was the Fourth of July by the sparks in his eyes as I touched my lips to his.

"Thank you, Laurie," he breathed as I pulled away.

Between the jeers and laughs, I whispered, "That's okay." I swear, I could hear Wendall's chest hair growing.

Star got to kiss Nathan. She winked at me when she had finished.

I kissed Bobby Carter. He tasted like cloves.

Nathan kissed Cora.

Lester and Wendall shook hands.

Lester kissed Cora.

I shook hands with Betty Weeks. Until that moment I hadn't even paid her any attention. Maybe it was because she was dressed rather plainly in a dove gray skirt and blouse. Maybe it was because she was sitting to the side and not speaking very much. Her handshake felt limp and cool like a spring perch; and she pulled away first, being careful not to look into my eyes.

Then Wendall and Cora both pulled out red candy sticks. He moved toward her and she puckered up for him, but Wendall had other ideas. Maybe the half dozen or so other girls he had kissed had inspired him, or maybe it was the way Cora looked that night. She was dressed in a deep green shift, and I think she was wearing lipstick in the familiar shade of "Flaming Flamingo." Whatever the reason, Wendall wasn't letting her go with a wet-lipped pucker. He grabbed Cora around her waist, pulled her to him, and planted his lips over hers as if he were siphoning gasoline.

Cora's back went stiff but only for a moment. Then she relaxed with a sigh and slipped her right arm around Wendall's neck.

The kids began to count, "One, two, three, four, . . ." That kiss made it to a whole minute, and when Wendall finally let Cora go, her lips and chin were bright pink from the smeared lipstick and her eyes were dancing a regular jig.

"This is a great party!" Wendall squealed as he passed the hat to Nathan.

I would have liked to have had more time to stare at Cora, but Nathan reached into the hat and got a yellow candy stick. At my turn I prayed mine would be yellow, so Cora wouldn't have been the only one to have fun, but it was green and matched Lester and I gave him a little peck and let it go at that.

To my horror, the yellow candy ended up in Betty's hand. She looked at it for a long moment before she waved it in Nathan's direction. Nathan smiled sheepishly and moved toward Betty. She slipped a long-fingered hand on his shoulder and her peaceful expression said she welcomed his approaching lips.

Maybe it was just me, but the whole room seemed to get quiet, and a little light seemed to be poised over Nathan's and Betty's heads as they touched flesh to flesh. The kiss itself was not very long, and didn't even earn a commotion, but what I saw there was too much for me to stand.

I got up and said, "I think it's about time we went home, Star."

Star stared up at me from her place in the circle on the floor. "It can't be any later than eight," she said.

"I'm tired," I said firmly.

Star got up with Lester's help, took me by the arm, and led me to the porch. "This is about Betty and Nathan, isn't it?"

"You can tell?" I asked.

"Your eyes are green with jealousy." Star straightened her skirt.

"No advice?"

Star put her hands on her hips, but before she could answer, Nathan was standing on the porch beside us. Lester came up behind him.

"What's going on?" Nathan asked, making his voice very deep.

"Nothing," I said quickly, suddenly ashamed of my envy.

"What's going on out here?" Wendall asked as he came to the door.

Star turned toward Wendall. "Laurie and I need to go home."

"Thank your mama for the good time," I said to Wendall.

"We'll walk with you to the crossroads," Nathan said.

Lester hurried inside and returned with two lanterns.

Star followed Lester off the porch. I followed Nathan after them. As I did another voice, a too sweet voice, asked, "Mind if I walk along with you?" It was Betty, and she was asking Nathan.

Nathan stopped abruptly and held out the lantern so Betty could catch up with us without falling over something in the yard. I felt a pang in my heart as if someone had stabbed it with a piece of broken yellow candy.

12

At the crossroads Nathan asked, "What road are you girls taking home?"

"We'll go by the Callihan farm," I said.

Nathan laughed and turned toward Betty as he said, "It's haunted, you know."

"Tell me about it," Betty whispered as she stepped closer to Nathan.

My heart began to beat faster as Nathan told about how Mr. Callihan had gone off drinking one night and returned home to find his wife and little children burned up in their sleep. About how he had gone out to the barn, the very place Star and I had visited after the juke joint, and hanged himself. And on and on about how legend had it that he appeared at the farm every full moon and walked about the place carrying a torch and calling for his wife and children.

Betty breathed deeply after the story and said, "Is that really, really true?"

I then realized my heart wasn't thumping out of fear — it was thumping out of anger toward Betty. I saw my chance and said, "I've seen the torch myself."

"You're so brave, Laurie," Nathan teased.

I knew Nathan's words were said in jest, but it hurt me that he made fun of me in front of Betty.

Lester handed a lantern to Star and said, "Guard the light carefully, you'll need it." He looked long at her and started to

120

speak, but Star kissed him on the cheek, turned, and walked into the dark woods.

I followed her. We hadn't gone twenty feet before the lantern flame was snuffed out by the wind.

Star said, "Let's go light the lantern before the kids get too far away."

We hurried back to the crossroads.

"Good, I see a light," Star said.

I eased around Star and saw only two people standing in the road. One of them was Nathan. He had his back to us, but I recognized his plaid shirt. The other one, looking directly into my soul, was Betty. She had her arms around Nathan's neck.

"I'll get the lantern lit," Star whispered. "You slip into the woods."

As Star spoke, Nathan and Betty shifted against each other in the glow from a lantern near them on the ground.

"The story you told was wonderful," Betty said with the voice of a nightingale.

Nathan laughed softly.

"I enjoyed your kiss," she sang.

Nathan slowly lowered Betty's arms and said, "I think we'd better hurry back. We told Lester we would be right behind him."

"Whatever you say," Betty said, taking hold of Nathan's arm.

Star coughed.

Betty turned toward Star with a triumphant look on her face. Nathan looked as if he were three years old and had been caught with his hand in the cookie jar.

I watched as Star lit our lantern from Nathan's lamp. I watched as she came toward me, and Nathan and Betty walked into the woods.

121

"If you say you warned me about Betty and Nathan, I'll take the lantern and leave you in the dark," I told Star.

Star didn't say anything. Instead, she gave me a hug and pointed toward the path.

There is something about the night that makes a person's blood turn to ice water. There is something about the night that makes a person's knees knock like a loose gate in the wind. There is something about the night that makes a person walk hand in hand with her aunt, waiting for the slightest sensation that tells her to run, run for her life.

"There's the old barn," Star said as we approached the Callihan farm.

Funny, the night Star and I rested there to get out of the rain the barn had said welcome. Now it said stay away, and I suspected that it meant it.

"We've come close enough," Star said.

"We can get out of here faster if we run across the garden."

"You're as crazy as a bedbug! Crazier! I'm not going anywhere near that garden."

"Oh, good grief! Then stay here. I'm not letting Nathan's bedtime story for Betty bother me. I'm taking the short cut." I waited to see what Star would do.

"Let's get it over with," Star finally said.

We started toward the old, overgrown garden. I could smell the scent of honeysuckle on the fence. There was also the rich odor of roses blooming across a rickety trellis.

Star moved toward the honeysuckle, then froze.

I looked beyond her to see a light, with the brilliance of a torch, coming toward us.

"You see it, don't you?" Star breathed.

"I see it," I said.

"It's Callihan, coming for the people who burned his house. He'll think we did it," Star said. "Let's get out of here."

We started walking, glancing back now and then to be certain the torch wasn't catching up with us. It kept a respectable distance for a while, but as we were approaching the low water bridge it suddenly seemed closer.

"Whoever is holding that torch knows the layout of this land," Star said. "He skipped the road and came down the bluff. I'd say he gained a half mile on us."

"Can we make it home before the torch gets to us?" I said, trying to catch my breath.

"It'll be a run for our lives," Star said.

We began to trot, then to canter, and finally to gallop like wild horses with a lariat at our necks. The torch appeared just beyond us, hovering waist-high at the edge of the woods.

Star reached down and picked up a stick. "You draw it out, and I'll bean it one," she instructed.

"You'd better not miss," I warned as I slipped down the trail, trying to walk as if I weren't afraid of the rotten, vengeful corpse of old Mr. Callihan waiting for me in the bushes.

I took a few steps and waited. The torch at my right moved. I could hear Star snapping twigs in the woods as she positioned herself for the ambush. Walk. Walk. Torch at my elbow. Star snapping branches. Walk. Walk. Torch at my face. Star flying through the air with a big stick in her hand.

"Don't! For land sakes, don't bop me with that tree!" the torchbearer cried.

Star pulled back the stick with about as much force as she had swung it at the torch. She looked at the night stalker, then at me.

Beneath the torch, with his face twisted in disbelief, was Willie Tate.

"What do you think you're doing, scaring us half to death?" I asked.

123

Willie didn't look at me. Instead he looked into Star's eyes and said, "I need to get Nan to come take a look at Grandma. She's ailing. She's been worried out of her mind, and it's doing her harm."

Star said to me, "Run. Get Nan."

I left them in the woods and hurried toward the lights of the house. Nannie and Mama met me on the back porch.

"We were about to come looking for you," Mama said.

"Where's Star?" Nannie asked as she peered into the darkness.

"Willie Tate's down the trail. He said his grandma is sick, and he needs you to come see about her," I said.

Nannie said, "Sarah, get my old suitcase with the medicines in it."

Mama hurried inside.

"Why doesn't Granny Yarrow go to the doctor?" I asked.

Nannie whispered, "Well, you know some folks think she's a witch, living down there in that swamp, elusive as a vapor. She wouldn't want just anyone poking and prodding around on her."

Star and Willie came into the yard at the same time Mama returned with the bag.

"We'll take the truck," Mama said. "No use getting Mr. Avartoz out of bed. Besides, he probably wouldn't want to drive his 'beloved automobile' that far into the swamp."

Mama fired up the truck, and she and Nannie got in. Willie, Star, and I got in the back, and we started toward the swamp on the lumber road. We traveled deep into the woods, deeper than I had ever gone. Past weeping willows, past rotting logs of great oaks, past marshland and bull rushes and goblins and trolls.

Star and Willie sat side by side, whispering to each other once in a while. I could tell they were friends, much greater friends than Star had wanted me to believe. Occasionally, in

124

the moonlight I could see the way Willie was looking at her, as if he thought she was beautiful. Star caught me looking at them and smiled. She had the eyes of a gypsy, sitting there beside the wild boy.

We got out of the truck where the road ended and walked single file along a small path. The ground beneath my feet oozed mud, and I could almost feel the leeches sizing me up for a midnight meal. The odors of wet moss and still water added to the feeling of loneliness.

I expected a shack at the end of the trail, but saw, instead, a small cottage, well lit with lamps. A big rocking chair took up most of the front porch; and a half dozen fat, yellow cats sat on the steps.

Willie ran ahead and called inside, "I brought Nan Gabriel."

Nannie was at Granny Yarrow's bedside before Willie had finished speaking.

I stood near the door with Mama and Star as Nannie bent over the old woman and placed her hand on Granny Yarrow's wrinkled brow.

"You don't have a fever," Nannie said softly.

Granny Yarrow scooted up to her elbows and stared at us. "Who's with you, Nan?"

"My daughters, Sarah and Star, and Laurie, Sarah's girl," Nannie said proudly.

"Put on some tea, Willie," Granny Yarrow said, motioning for Willie to get the pot going.

"You don't need to entertain us," Nannie said. "We came to see if you were all right."

Granny Yarrow sat up and swung her feet off the bed. "Don't get much company way out here. Think I'd best be sociable when I have some."

Mama hurried to help Granny Yarrow get things ready. As they prepared the tea party I took a good look at the room.

125

The place was not damp and dark as I had expected. It was alive with color and with the fine handiwork of lace. There were lace coverlets on the furniture, lace curtains, lace around old photographs. Hundreds of yards of handmade lace.

And on one wall, hung on pegs, were several of the finest dulcimers I had ever seen. Some were made of cherry, others of walnut; and one was made of a black wood, so black it glistened.

Granny Yarrow must have sensed where I was looking because she said, "That dark dulcie came from Germany. I think it's a cedar found only in the northern forests. My great-grandfather brought it with him to America. He made the dulcie himself." She took a dulcimer of cherry wood off the shelf and handed it to me. Then she took a walnut one for herself, and we sat down.

"I heard you play, girl," Granny Yarrow said. "Listen to this little tune. It came from my grandmother's side of the family. She was from England, you see." She began to play a sweet melody. It was built on single notes with a rhythm I could easily feel.

Nannie sat down beside Granny Yarrow and began to hum.

When they were done, Nannie said, "Willie thought you were sick. It appears there is nothing wrong with your body. What's the matter?"

Granny Yarrow sighed and sat down in a chair beside the door. "They're going to build that shoe factory, you know."

"I know," Nannie said.

"It takes up a pretty fair piece of the swamp," Granny Yarrow said.

"It does," Nannie agreed, "but it shouldn't come back here."

Granny Yarrow looked at her hands. "I don't own this piece of land or this house."

"Who owns it?" Nannie asked.

126

"Rhetta Harper has the rights, and folks are going to know it if those surveyors finish their job and measure off the place," Granny Yarrow said.

Mama asked, "How did you come to live here?"

"Mr. Harper gave it to me when I first came to Guthrie since I was living alone and had Willie to raise. Mr. Harper felt pity for me having that burden and no way to make a living. Rhetta was never to know. People might have talked. 'Course, there would have been nothing to it, but who would have believed a woman living to herself in the swamp."

"Surely Rhetta wouldn't have an interest in this place," Mama said.

"I just don't know," Granny Yarrow said.

Nannie said, "You put the worrying aside. I'll see to it you don't have to leave your home."

Granny Yarrow jumped up, grabbed Nannie's hands, and held them to her chest. "May the good Lord bless and keep you," she said.

Star and I got in the back of the truck when we started home. I heard Mama and Nannie talking as we drove away. Nannie said, "I'll deal with Rhetta. I'm afraid I'm the one who has talked about security and keeping hold of what we have all these years. Rhetta will find it hard to give up a piece of property with her name on it."

"Funny how little things bother a person so when an honest conversation could solve the problem," Mama said.

Nannie didn't say anything more.

Star scooted next to me and laid her head on my shoulder.

"What's wrong?" I asked her. "Do you have one boyfriend too many?"

Before Star could answer, Mama tapped on the window between the front seat and ours and smiled at me. Then she put her arm around Nannie.

127

13

Although most barn raisings, corn huskings, and other such parties usually didn't take place until the crops were laid by, raising the rafters on the shoe factory edged out even hay making in the community's eyes.

There was going to be a box-lunch auction at the factory dedication, so it was important for me to prepare a meal that would impress Nathan. I wasn't certain why impressing him even mattered. He seemed perfectly happy escorting Betty in the moonlight. Maybe I just wanted to beat her at something.

Star and I used the same white paper decorated with hearts for our box lunches. I chose to pack fried chicken with lemon pie. Star chose roast beef sandwiches and oatmeal cookies.

It was custom to keep the identity of the owner of each box secret, but girls were known to whisper something to their beaus about how their box was decorated. Then their boyfriends would bid the most on it, and the couple would get to eat the meal together.

I tied my box with a red bow, and Star tied hers with a white bow so there wouldn't be any confusion at bidding time.

There was also a "beauty" cake to be given away. Elsie Neilson always baked that cake. She used a recipe for cream cake her grandmother had brought with her from Sweden. The recipe called for fresh coconut milk, which was hard to come by, but Mrs. Neilson knew several places she could order coconuts from, even in the middle of summer.

Everyone would stand around one of Mrs. Neilson's cakes and mutter, "Wonder how she does it?"

Someone else would say, "She knows someone over in 'Hawayah.'"

"Down in them islands, missionaries send them to her," another would add.

Mrs. Neilson never told her secret of gathering the fresh coconuts, but she continued to bake the cakes.

Star and I rode out early to the shoe factory site with Mr. Avartoz. Nannie and Mama were coming out later on a flatbed truck Al Graham had arranged to hold all the boarders, including Ezra in his new wheelchair.

When we arrived we sneaked our box lunches to the auction table under a grove of sycamores and admired Mrs. Neilson's cake. I noticed that the beauty contest jars beside it, collecting votes at a penny each, already had some coins in them. There were ten jars in all, including one for me and one for Star. Betty Weeks had a jar. Even Cora had a jar with her name on it. It had two pennies in it. One of the coins looked as if it had been pried out of cement.

A lot of other young people were already there, standing around and giggling. The boys kept jingling the change in their pockets, and the girls kept hanging onto their arms, secretly hoping, I knew, that the boy of their choice had brought enough hard cash to ensure they would dine together, instead of with old bachelors and fat cousins.

Nathan was in the group. I walked over to him and said, "How's it going?"

"All right," he said softly. He glanced toward where the wagons, trucks, and automobiles were being parked in the field.

Star hurried toward us. "Have you seen Lester?" she asked Nathan.

Nathan answered quickly, "They aren't here yet."

He had said *they*. *They* with a familiar tone to it. *They* as a word that stood for someone. Someone special.

Star said, "There they are."

"*They* are here," I said, mockingly.

"I see that," Nathan said as he walked to where Mr. Weeks was parking his automobile.

"You two!" Star said as she followed him.

Cora was waiting beside the box-lunch table, so I walked over to stand by her.

"There's going to be a whole passel of contests," Cora said, smiling.

I didn't speak.

She continued, "Prizes for the longest married couple, the largest family, the ugliest man, the prettiest baby, the most people in a wagon, the man with the longest beard, the largest married couple, the dirtiest little boy, the tug-of-war, the greased pole climbing contest, and the winner of the fat man's footrace."

"Sounds exciting," I said.

"And an overland race for the young people. Mr. Thomas has put up a dollar prize, in candy and soda, for the winner," Cora said. "Mama's in charge of it all." A quick answer to why Cora had a jar in the beauty cake contest.

Wendall Taylor walked toward us. Cora began to straighten her hair. "Do I look all right?" she asked.

"It's only Wendall," I assured her.

"I know," she said sweetly.

I could see the kiss at Wendall's party had done something for Cora. I left the two of them together and walked over to stand by Mama. She had just gotten off Al Graham's truck.

"What are you doing standing around?" she asked me. "Why aren't you with your friends?"

"I don't fit in anymore," I heard myself say.

130

"Problems with Nathan?"

"He doesn't want me to go away and sing," I said.

"What do you want to do, Laurie?"

"I like the idea of being on stage, but I also like it here in Guthrie."

"You'll have to decide sometime, sweetie," Mama said. "Chances are, pretty soon." She patted me on the cheek and walked over to help Nannie settle the boarders on the benches that had been set up in the shade.

I continued to stand there, feeling invisible, until someone asked, "Going to play?"

It was Nathan. His voice sounded strained, and Betty was standing only a few feet behind him.

"Thought I'd watch," I said.

"You've always played games," he said.

"My dress is fresh-washed." I smoothed my skirt.

Nathan looked away, then back, then toward Betty, then into my eyes. "Come on and help us pile down a wagon. Most people in one win soda pop. You won't get your dress mussed." He held out his hand to me.

"You two go on. I'll be there directly," I said.

Nathan turned and walked with Betty toward the young people who were getting ready to climb into a wagon.

I dragged along behind them and stood while the others got in: Star and Lester, Cora and Wendall, Betty and Nathan. I started to tremble and assured myself that I *did* like games. Nathan reached out for me again, and this time I took his hand and let him pull me up beside him in the wagon.

We won the soda pop. The bottles were handed out at random. I got a cream soda, which I absolutely hated. I gave it to Bo-Henry after he stood beside me for five minutes, drooling over it. Betty got a strawberry, which she sipped and made her rosebud lips even pinker.

131

Nathan knew a lot about me. He was right; I did like games. But after a brief look at Betty's charmed face, I realized the only games I really liked were those I could win.

I sat on a bench in the shade with Nannie for most of the other contests. The winners were pretty standard. Elvira and Tab White always won the prize for the fattest couple. "Prettiest Baby" went to the mayor's granddaughter. She had won the contest last year, but they kept raising the age of contestants so she would still be eligible. It got a little more interesting with the "Dirtiest Little Boy" contest. This was the first year the local boys were given a run for their money by Rah-Rah Weeks. Apparently, Rah-Rah had been down by the river rolling in the mud right before the judging. The only parts of him that weren't soiled were his big, white eyeballs.

When Mrs. Weeks saw her little darling caked in mud and as black as a cinder, she grabbed her chest and fanned her face with a large, lace handkerchief. Rah-Rah took the prize of a sack of licorice whips and ran away to hide from his mama.

Mr. Weeks apparently thought Rah-Rah was pretty funny. He was laughing as he came toward us. He lowered himself onto our quilt as if he were a heavy sack of potatoes. "I don't mean to interrupt your merrymaking, Sarah, but I did want to take the time to thank you for your contribution to the factory," Mr. Weeks said.

Mama smiled. "I'm behind you one hundred percent."

Mr. Weeks looked away for a moment, then said, "I know you are." He then glanced at Nannie, smiled at me, and got up slowly.

"Wonder what that was all about?" Nannie asked after Mr. Weeks had joined his family by the picnic tables.

"He's grateful to Mama," I said, but I wondered why he didn't seem happier on the day set aside for him.

132

Nannie looked long at Mama before she said, "I suppose."

"Time to eat," someone called, so we got up and walked toward the table covered with the box lunches.

"Who'll give me a dollar for this beautiful box lunch?" Al Graham called to the crowd.

It was Cora's box. She had pointed it out to me earlier.

I searched for Cora. She was standing to the side of the picnic area, looking exceptionally sweet.

Wendall Taylor bellowed, "I'll give a whole dollar."

Someone else said, "I'll give a dollar and a quarter."

I suspected that the second bidder had been planted in the crowd to keep the bids high. I couldn't figure out who else would want to eat lunch with Cora.

"Wendall, are you going to raise that to a dollar fifty?" Al asked.

Wendall said, "Yes, sir!"

Al said, "We have a dollar fifty. Do I hear more?"

From the back, "Two dollars."

Wendall turned toward Cora with a look of horror on his face. He mouthed, "I only have a dollar fifty."

Cora smiled weakly.

Al brought the gavel down and said, "Sold to Cora's brother."

Cora's smile snapped like a twig in an ice storm when that line reached her ears. Peter was right beside Aunt Nola and they had superior looks on their faces as if they had just righted a great wrong.

Cora plowed through the crowd to get them, and with a voice that could be heard at the bottom of a well, said, "Why under God's Heaven did you bid on my box? Wendall only had —" She suddenly stopped talking and stepped away from Peter and her mother. "Mama, you didn't want me to have my meal with Wendall, did you?"

133

Before Aunt Nola could say anything, Cora sprinted into the woods. Peter walked to the table, paid for the box lunch, and pulled out a chicken leg to gnaw on.

Poor Wendall stood beside his mama with his dollar fifty in his hand, looking bewildered. He turned to look at Aunt Nola. With heavy steps, he moved toward her.

"What is it, Wendall?" Aunt Nola asked. She glanced toward Peter, who was still devouring food out of Cora's lunch box.

"You shouldn't oughta have done that. I brought my money. I saved it up for that box. I wanted to have lunch with Cora," Wendall said hoarsely.

"Now, Wendall, really, we're not here to merely have *lunch*. We're here to raise the walls on this shoe factory. Why, some of the men are already at work. Don't you think you should hurry along and help out? I'm sure they could use your strong muscles." Aunt Nola reached out and tweaked Wendall's arm.

He pulled away. "I think maybe I'll use my strong muscles to rip down those boards. Who needs an old shoe factory? We were plenty happy without it. Everyone got along all right. That's not saying Cora is feeling all right, is it? She's run off. Down in the swamp, probably crying. Little you care. Telling her what to think. Telling her what to do all the time. You can have your old shoe factory any day. I hope a twister carries it away!" With that said, Wendall hurried into the woods, probably to find Cora. I had never heard him say so many words in his entire life.

I felt as if I should applaud or something. But I just stood quietly like everyone else until Al Graham said, "Next box."

That box belonged to Cindy Fletcher, in from the hills. It sold for seventy-five cents to her fiancé. They walked away arm in arm to share it under a shady elm.

Four other lunches were sold before Al picked up Star's

134

box. I was standing by Star and Lester. They were both beaming.

"I'll pay a dollar for that box," Lester said.

"But, son, I haven't even asked for a bid," Al teased.

Lester blushed and smiled.

"Do I hear another bid?" Al asked.

From the back of the crowd a surly voice said, "Two dollars."

I turned to see who it was, but the winners of the fattest couple contest were blocking the entire horizon.

"Two fifty," Lester said. His face had turned pale.

A voice moving toward the front said, "Three dollars." It was Willie Tate, as big as life, followed by his friend Alvin.

"I don't believe it," Star said softly.

"I said three dollars," Willie repeated. He came to stand by Lester.

Lester chirped, "Three fifty."

"Four dollars," Willie said. "Four dollars for the box of Shining Star."

Some of the kids behind us laughed and drew a piercing glare from Star.

"Four fifty," Lester said.

"Tired of playing around," Willie said. "I'm bidding it all. Eight dollars in hard cash." He held up a hand full of bills and turned to stare into Lester's peaked face.

Lester swallowed so hard that I heard it.

Star said, "Bid what you have, honey. Willie has spent his wad."

Lester said, "I don't have over eight dollars."

Star screamed, "WHAT? You're loaded. Your daddy *owns* this shoe factory."

Willie moved toward Star. "Looks like old moneybags let you down. I'll never let you down. Don't you know that by

135

now, Shining Star?" He spoke softly, as if he wanted only Star to hear him.

"Don't call me that," Star spat.

"Let her be," I said to Willie.

He turned toward me. "Well, if it isn't the little saint. Seems we were all having a pretty good time around here until you wandered back."

"Shut up," Star said.

Lester just stood with his hands in his pockets.

Willie said, "Now, Shining Star, I'm about tired of you saying one thing to me by moonlight and another by blazing sun. And if you were counting on this fellow taking you away from Guthrie, I bet you're in for a big letdown. You don't belong with his kind. You belong with me. We're alike. Isn't that right?"

"I don't know why you're treating me this way, embarrassing me in front of all these people," Star said. Her voice was frail, and she was shaking.

Willie glanced around, blushing a little. "I wanted you to be my girl, that's all." He scuffed the toe of his worn boot in the dirt.

Star turned to leave, but Willie grabbed her arm. She shoved him away, saying, "Don't you ever touch me without asking first!"

He grabbed her again. She shoved him hard enough so that he landed with a thud on the ground. Star turned and ran into the woods.

Nannie weaved through the crowd. "Chase her down," Nannie said to me as she bent over to take care of Willie.

I ran after Star. Between Cora and her, the woods were full of kin.

136

14

It wasn't hard to find Star's path through the timber. It seemed as if she were headed to the bluff above Blackie's Rock on the Wigerstat. I should have asked Nathan to come with me, but my pride stuck in my throat like a grindstone and kept me from it. So I tracked alone, except for the chiggers and ticks that were falling off the trees onto me in hopes of a free lunch.

When the lumber mill had been in operation, many of the paths in the woods had been used by the millers to transport logs to the bluff above the river. There they had made chutes down the mountainside, where ties were shoved into the river. From there crews ran the banks and, with long poles, guided the floating lumber downstream until it could be loaded onto barges. The river from that point to the dam was still full of sinkers, green logs that had not seasoned enough to float, and huge iron hooks used to tow the logs.

Star seemed to be running toward the main chute. It was a dangerous place, often slick with mud. Some of the bigger boys liked to hang out there and slide down the chute into the river.

Nannie had caught Star and me there a few years back and switched us for being so careless in our play. A preacher, supposedly reading his Bible as he rode through the woods, had been lost over the bluff when his mule took a step too far to the side.

I began to worry about what Star was planning to do.

"Help," I heard. It sounded like the voice of a small child.

"Where are you?" I asked.

Again a weak "Help."

I ran toward the bluff, eased to the edge, and peeked over the side. I could see the river churning below. It was a fifty-foot drop to jagged rock. I saw no one. As I stepped back the voice said, "We're here. We're tucked in under the bluff."

"Who?" I asked the wind.

"It's me, Star, and Cora. Cora's holding on to my foot. I'm afraid to move. She'll crash," Star said.

I could hear whimpering. It had to be coming from Cora.

"I'll get help," I said.

"No time," Star answered.

"I can't reach you," I said. "I can't even see you."

"It will be too late," Star said.

But I turned and ran through the woods. It was only a little ways back, wasn't it? No, how long had I been walking? Ten minutes? Twenty minutes? How long? The branches slapped against my face. The brambles tore at my ankles. I could hear someone crashing through the woods. Please, God, let it be Wendall and his big bear arms. Please, God, Star and I are sorry for all those times we prayed that Cora would fall over a cliff. Please, help us.

It wasn't Wendall. It was Nannie and Aunt Nola.

"Quick, Star and Cora are over the bluff, barely holding on," I said. I turned and ran.

Nannie and Aunt Nola came charging behind me. At the bluff we all stopped and listened.

"Is that you, Laurie?" Star asked.

"Where are they?" Nannie asked.

Star yelled, "That you, Nan? Oh, God, thank you!"

Aunt Nola was all action then. "Nan, you lie on your

138

stomach and hook your feet around that old oak. Grab hold of my legs and lower me over the side of the bluff."

"Headfirst?" Nannie asked.

"I can get a look-see and know what we're up against," Aunt Nola said. She turned to me. "Laurie, you get on your stomach beside me. Hold on to my waist and let's peek."

Nannie did as Aunt Nola said and lay on her stomach and secured her feet around the oak. She latched onto her sister's feet as tightly as a mama cat carrying a kitten across a rafter.

I lay on my stomach beside Aunt Nola and hooked my left arm through her right elbow. We eased over the bluff. There, on the tiniest of ledges, was Star. Holding on to Star's foot and dangling over the water was Cora.

Without a word Aunt Nola stood up and ripped off her skirt. She was back over the bluff in a moment. I eased beside her to help her balance as she passed one end of the cloth to Star.

"Help Cora catch the fabric. I'll pull her up," Aunt Nola said.

Cora took the fabric and began to whirl upward with the help of Star, Aunt Nola, and me. Nannie held on to Aunt Nola. As Cora's head appeared, I reached out and grabbed her, pulling her to safety.

Star was next. She was clinging to a piece of root extended above her head.

"We'll pull you up," Aunt Nola had just said when Star screamed.

We looked over the bluff in time to see the tiny ledge disappear into a mud slide. Star was dancing along the side of the cliff and trying to hold onto the root, but she couldn't and in a swish began to slide toward the rocks and the river.

Aunt Nola was a cat. A pouncing mountain lion. She slid over the bluff so quickly I didn't know what was going on until I saw her big hands grasping tufts of grass and disappearing into the air. I lay on my stomach and watched as she moved her weight slowly through the mud, easing down on her stomach until Star could grab her foot. Then she started back up. Slowly, digging into the ground, clawing at it with her nails, pulling the two of them up with a strength that must have come from the very Heaven she was always trying to do good by.

At the top, Nannie and Cora and I wrestled Aunt Nola to safety. Star came along with her with a strange look in her eyes and great tears flowing down her cheeks.

Star got on her knees and grabbed Aunt Nola around the legs. "Thank you, thank you so much. Before God I'm saying I'm going to be a better person. I have tasted the bitterness of death and I never want to do that again. Forgive me for everything I ever said unkind to you."

I expected Aunt Nola to praise God for the repentance, but, instead, she scooped Star into her arms and held her.

We missed lunch. I didn't even know who bought my box. I would have bet it wasn't Nathan. Whoever it was ate alone, as did Willie Tate. Imagine paying eight dollars for roast beef sandwiches and oatmeal cookies.

We would have gone on home, but there was to be a dedication ceremony, some entertainment, and a speech by Mr. Weeks. We sat at the back of the crowd on an old quilt. Several people stopped by to ask us why we were all so dirty, and Nannie told them we'd had "a little accident in the woods" and let it go at that.

Nathan was more persistent in his questioning. He sat down beside me and asked, "What really happened out there?"

I tried not to look at him as I said, "Star and Cora fell over the bluff. It took a while to get them."

"You're fooling with me," Nathan said.

I turned toward him, and we looked into each other's eyes. I noticed that Nathan had a scratch on his face. He must have seen that I noticed it because he touched it and said, "Got my scar during the overland race."

"Did you win?"

He smiled. "Of course. And you won the beauty cake."

"Very funny."

"Really. By about the two dollars I put in it."

"I thought that cake would be on the Weekses' kitchen table by nightfall."

Nathan stood up quickly.

There would have been more to the conversation, but Hiram Lawson came over to me and said, "Laurie girl, would you sing a few songs for us? Mr. Weeks has gone with some of the men to walk around the property. We need to keep the folks interested in the doings."

I glanced at Mama. She smiled and said, "It's your life. I told you there would be decisions."

"I look a mess," I told her.

"You'll sound just fine," Nannie said with unusual enthusiasm.

I nodded at Hiram, and he hurried back to announce my upcoming performance from the makeshift stage someone had hammered together.

I begged a guitar off Willis Young. It was an ancient flattop with the wood worn to a patina by callused fingers. It seemed like just the right instrument to welcome a factory.

As Hiram helped me up on the stage, I turned to see Nathan step toward the edge of the woods. Betty got up from beside her mother on a bench and walked over to him. I might as well have been hammering the nails in the coffin of my own love life as I strummed that guitar and sang a verse of "Sourwood Mountain."

141

It was the first time I realized I would never be able to please everyone in my life. I could see Mama smiling at me; she was pleased. Nannie was smiling slightly; she was happy for me. Star was ignoring me; she would be sad to see me go. Nathan was pretending I had never existed.

The people were smiling and clapping and singing along with me. I sang "Little Log Cabin in the Lane" and "I'm Nobody's Darling on Earth." They begged for more. I *would* be on the stage. I *would* be on the radio.

I entertained until Mr. Weeks arrived with the other men. Then I got down and went to sit by Mama and Nannie.

Mr. Weeks walked to the center stage, cleared his throat, and said, "Thank you for coming here today . . . neighbors." His voice wavered when he said "neighbors."

Everyone sat still, waiting to hear magic words.

"Thank you for building this fine frame."

Silence.

"Thank you for wanting progress."

A baby began to cry.

"The factory will be finished soon, and we'll all be working."

The people clapped, slowly at first and then thunderously. It was followed by more slow, molasses silence.

"That's all I have to say," Mr. Weeks finished. He jumped off the stage and hurried to hold his wife's hand.

"That speech was like a fireworks display that fizzled," Mr. Avartoz said as he began to help the other boarders get up to walk to Al Graham's truck.

Star and I began to gather our quilts and picnic baskets. A man in a rumpled gray suit came toward me. "Laurie? Laurie Hargrove?" he asked.

"Yes," I said.

"I'm Eric Houser. Your mother was expecting me."

142

Mama was at my side then, extending her hand to the stranger. She turned to me. "Laurie, this is the man from WSB in Atlanta. The one I arranged an audition with."

The man smiled at me. "I hope you didn't mind me hearing you like this. I had business at Buck's Point and heard about the dedication. I knew if this girl was going to be anyone, she'd be singing today."

"What did you think?" Mama asked.

"Wonderful. Absolutely wonderful," he said softly.

My heart was beating so fast I knew he could hear it.

He reached out and took my hand. "I'll finish my business and be back in a couple of days. We'll work out something then."

Star had heard it all. As the man left, she, too, turned and walked away. She returned in a minute with the beauty cake. "Looks like you win everything today, Laurie," she said as she handed the cake to me.

We went to bed early, and I dozed off thinking about the possibility of going to Atlanta. I was awakened by someone calling my name. I opened my eyes to see Star staring out the window.

"What is it?"

"Do you suppose those are the flames of Hell?" she asked.

I hurried to the window and gasped.

Star turned and ran into the hall, calling, "Nan! Nan! There's a fire! Beyond the ridge!"

The old stand of white pines along the bluff was silhouetted like a field of corn shocks before a harvest moon.

I pulled on my wrap and hurried to the front porch, where the boarders had gathered. Mr. Avartoz was still dressed. Most of the others were pulling things on over their nightclothes.

"It's the shoe factory," Mr. Avartoz breathed.

Nannie said, "I believe you're right. God help us all."

There was a collective sigh.

"Our dreams . . . gone up in smoke," Apples added.

Another sigh.

"Nan, you coming with me?" Mr. Avartoz asked as he stepped off the porch and toward the barn.

Mama appeared at the door, "Oh, my dear Lord!" she cried.

"Dress, girls, we need to get on over there and help out," Nannie said as she followed Mr. Avartoz to the barn to get the shovels and saws and burlap bags they kept stored for just such emergencies.

At first, Mama didn't move. She stood in the moonlight and stared at the flames. Then she slowly opened her hands toward Heaven, as if she were releasing a dove.

I started toward Mama, to hug her, but Mrs. Turner appeared at the door. She was screaming. Her stiff, white hair was floating around her face as if she had on a veil. "Help me. Save me!" she cried as she stared at the fire beyond the hill.

"You're in no danger," Nehemiah said flatly.

"I could burn up," Mrs. Turner said in desperation. She went to Apples, then to Nehemiah, and lastly to Mama. "You'll help me, won't you, Sarah girl?"

I knew Mama liked games. Mama liked pretend. But Mama also liked the reality of a script, and Mrs. Turner's scene had no certain ending. I nearly gasped when Mama said, "I'll go upstairs and put you to bed, Mrs. Turner." She put her arm around Mrs. Turner's shoulders and escorted her into the house.

Star and I ran upstairs to pull on the dungarees we wore when we worked in the garden.

"What do you suppose happened at the factory?" I asked.

Star breathed deeply.

"It was probably set," I added.

144

"You don't know that. It could have been a cigaroot. The flick of an ash," she said quickly.

"It's too wet for that. Even the woods are still muddy."

"There's always some danger in putting people together and shaking them up like a can of hornets. Someone is bound to get stung." She sounded distant.

"What's wrong?" I asked. "You've been angry with me ever since Mr. Houser showed up."

Star stuffed her dungarees into the tops of her short boots, ignoring my question.

I plopped down on the bed and tried to lace my shoes. I started to sniffle. It was awful. I couldn't keep from wiping at my face, and I knew I needed to hurry.

Star was there in a minute, on her knees, tying my shoes in much the same way she had when I was too little to do it myself.

"I love you, Star," I whispered.

She looked up at me with sad eyes and said, "You know I love you, too."

Nannie's calling for us to hurry made us jump, and we bolted for the door.

"Who would have torched the factory?" I asked as we hurried down the hall.

Star didn't say anything as she ran ahead.

"Could it have been —"

"Hush up," she cut in. "Don't put any names with the crime. There will be plenty of talk without you adding to it."

"This is between you and me."

"Not here," Star said, scoffing, "not in Guthrie. Even the trees are alive. They have ears. They have tongues."

I followed her to Mama's truck, got in, and kept my thoughts to myself as we rode toward the fire and watched the forest bleed and heard it sigh.

145

15

The picnic the day before the fire didn't have nearly the clout at pulling the community together as that fire did. We stood shoulder to shoulder in a long line and passed buckets of swamp water to the men nearest the fire.

Our family included Aunt Nola, Peter, Cora, Nannie, Mama, Star, myself, and our boarders: Mr. Avartoz, Apples, and old, rickety Nehemiah. Other families made up other links in the chain. Old people stood next to young people. Strong young men stood beside weak old men.

"We ain't going to be able to save it!" someone called in a desperate voice.

I think we all knew that was a fact even as we unloaded the truck and started working. The fire was lapping at the building frame like a wolf drooling over a lamb.

Nannie set down her bucket, and we all did as she did. I stood beside Mama to watch the rafters collapse. Star stood beside Nannie. Quietly, Nannie slipped her arm around Star's shoulders and pulled her close. People voiced their regrets and invited each other home for breakfast.

Watching this all from behind blackened faces were Mr. and Mrs. Weeks. They both looked as if they had lost their best friends, and I last saw them being helped to an automobile by the mayor.

"It'll be hard on the Weekses," Nannie said as we put our tools in the truck.

146

"It'll be hard on all of us," Mama said. She motioned for me to come to her.

I threw my arms around Mama.

Mama said, "We'll have to start over, honey."

"We'll all have to start over," Al Graham said as he walked toward us. "We can make it. We're a tough bunch." He smiled.

"Opportunity can knock, but it can also knock you in the head," Mama said to Al.

"Life's what you make it," Al said as he turned to leave.

Nannie slowly walked to Mama and slipped her arm around Mama's waist. Mama leaned against Nannie and sighed.

"Al's right," Nannie said. "Life is what you make it."

No one said anything more as we got in the truck.

I took a last glance at the building site as we drove away. The only damage to the woods was to the ring of pines around the clearing. The trees had been felled into heaps and looked like an old man's hands folded in death.

The meeting that took place in our front yard the next night was grim.

"Guess we know who did it," some man with a gruff voice said.

"Damn kids!" another man shouted.

Star and I heard it all from the parlor. We sat in the dark and listened, being unwelcome as children.

"We've decided on some suspects," Mr. Roth said.

I could see him sitting at his desk, poring over the names in his grade books to see who he hated enough to hang a crime on.

"Let's bring them before us and get this problem cleared up, once and for all," someone said.

"Arrest them?" another voice asked. "You know we'd have to get the law from over at Buck's Point."

"Let whoever did this come in on his own. Give him a chance to do right by us," Nannie said.

"Wendall will come in on his own," Al Graham said.

"Wendall?" I said loudly.

Star said, "Hush!"

"What about the others?" a woman asked.

"Yeah, Granny Yarrow has been seen slipping around the factory site for over a month now. And that grandson of hers, Willie, is a no-good. He won't show up over here. Have to get the law on his tail and drag him out of that swamp," a deep-voiced man said.

"Willie has as much right to come in on his own as Wendall does. He's innocent until proven guilty," Mama said.

Star moved closer to the window.

A man said, "Sarah, you're taking up for that no-good because he's sweet on Star."

Nannie answered, "She's taking up for him because we have no proof he did anything wrong." Her voice was firm.

Star eased away from the window and stood up.

"What are you doing?" I asked.

She stepped toward the parlor door. "I have to see someone."

"I don't think that's such a good idea . . ."

She turned quickly and disappeared down the hall.

I followed her upstairs and watched her change into her dungarees. "Are you going to find Willie? Are you going to warn him?" I asked.

"I'm just going out." She pulled on her oxfords.

"If he had the nerve to burn the factory, there's no telling what else he might do —"

"Willie didn't burn the factory."

"How do you know?"

148

"I just know. He might be a bigmouth, but he's not a firebug."

"That leaves Wendall. He told everyone he hoped a twister would blow the factory away."

"Wendall didn't do it either. Don't you know Wendall better than that? He wouldn't hurt a flea."

"He squeezed my arm real tight once," I said.

"He was probably only loving on you. He couldn't burn something this town holds as great a value in as that factory."

"Then who did it?" I asked as Star moved toward the window.

She didn't answer that question but said instead, "If need be, you'll cover for me with Nan, won't you?"

"I always have," I said to her shadow.

I made coffee and sat in the kitchen until everyone went home. The only light was in the hall. When Nannie came into the kitchen, she stopped suddenly as if I had startled her, then she poured herself a cup of coffee in the twilight with a deftness that came from knowing every inch of her own home.

Nannie sat down beside me and took a sip from her cup. "Where's Star?" she asked as if she knew I was waiting for the question.

"I saw her earlier," I said.

Nannie took another sip of coffee.

We sat in silence.

Finally, Mama came in, looked around, and asked, "Did Star go to warn Willie?"

"I think so," I said. "Don't you think you'd better go after her?"

Mama started toward the door, then turned toward Nannie. "Nan, I think you should be the one to find her. She's been sneaking out, and you've known it. She needs you to go after her."

149

"I have to tuck in the boarders. I need my rest. I'll never be able to get breakfast and fix lunch for everyone before church," Nannie said quickly.

Mr. Avartoz and Apples were in the kitchen then, and they had heard it all.

"You have a family," Apples said dramatically. "They share you with us all the time, take a little time for them."

"She's speaking the truth," Mr. Avartoz said.

"Breakfast?" Nannie asked.

"I'll fix it," Apples said.

Mama looked as startled as a falling cat.

Nannie stood up and walked to the door. "Too much change for an old woman," she mumbled as she hurried into the darkness toward the truck. If anyone could find Star, she would. There was determination in her walk.

The hearing concerning who burned the factory was held at two o'clock the next day. The early afternoon air had a tang to it, something like cider as it turns to vinegar. By one-thirty there were over a hundred people at the Community Building.

Mayor Brown, Mr. Roth, Al Graham, and Mr. Weeks filed in. They sat down behind a long table set near the front of the room.

Directly to their right were some chairs set up for the accused. Seated in the front row was Wendall Taylor. He was dressed in new overalls with a white shirt and tie. He had shaved his stubble of a beard and actually looked quite handsome.

Wendall's mother was seated beside him. She looked really old. Her face was as gray and hard-looking as slate, and she was bug-eyed and perched on the edge of her chair.

There was no sign of Willie Tate.

After the crowd had settled, Mayor Brown said, "Let's get this business over with so we can all get home to our dinners."

150

He turned toward Wendall and said, "Mr. Taylor, I believe you have something to say to us."

Wendall stood up and walked boldly toward his accusers. The only noise in the room came from whimpering babies.

"Speak your piece," Mayor Brown said.

Wendall looked directly ahead and said, "I didn't burn the building."

That was it.

"Were you at home that night, Wendall?" the mayor asked.

Wendall didn't speak.

Mayor Brown looked toward Mrs. Taylor and asked, "Was Wendall home that night?"

Mrs. Taylor answered, "Can't say."

Mayor Brown got up and stood beside Wendall. "Son, were you home that night?"

"I didn't burn the building," Wendall said again.

"You weren't home, were you?" the mayor asked.

Wendall didn't answer.

"Where were you?" Mayor Brown persisted.

Back and forth it went.

"I didn't burn the building."

"But you were out. Where were you?"

"I didn't do it."

"How do we know?"

"I didn't do it."

"Where were you?"

Wendall began to sob, holding his great bear hands over his face.

From the back of the room came a voice, crisp and clear, "He was with me."

It was so quiet you could have heard a bee sneeze.

Cora walked to the front, being careful to choose her path on the side of the room opposite Aunt Nola.

Mayor Brown whispered, "He was with you?"

"At the old barn on the Callihan's property," Cora said.

"Is that right, Wendall?" Mayor Brown asked.

Wendall didn't speak to the mayor, but said to Cora, "You didn't have to come up here."

"Yes, I did." She comforted Wendall as she took his hand into hers. She turned to the people, looked at her mother, and said, "It isn't what you think. Wendall and I don't play patty-cake or anything like that. I've been teaching him how to read and study and do better. That's all. We've worked together one night a week for about two years. We didn't think it would look proper doing it in front of everyone. I suppose we were wrong. But I want you to know I'm proud of Wendall. He is a fine man, and I hope to get to know him better."

Wendall smiled suddenly. "You mean I can court you?"

"You'll have to ask my mama," Cora said to him as if there were no one else in the room.

They walked, hand in hand, to stand beside Aunt Nola. When they got there, Aunt Nola, surprisingly, threw her arms around them and give them a hug.

It was the end of Act I.

I leaned toward Star and whispered, "Well, I never would have thought Cora had it in her to —"

Star sobbed.

I couldn't believe it. She was spouting leaks like a rain barrel hit by a buckshot.

"Hanky, quick!" I said to Mama.

Mama took one look at Star and scooted me aside to sit by her. They began to whisper to each other.

Cora's actions had touched some nerve in Star. Star couldn't stop crying. Nannie tried to comfort her, but even that didn't help.

I began to suspect Star's weeping was for Willie since he was the only person still accused. His absence from the

152

meeting almost declared his guilt. I was about to pronounce him "tried and hanged" when he sauntered into the room.

"Would you look at that," Mama said, marveling.

Willie took a shuffle step forward and then another back to the door. He extended his hand toward the front porch, and Granny Yarrow took it. He guided her inside as if she were the queen of England.

You could hear the prayers being offered and the four-leaf clovers being stroked for protection from the "witch."

Yet Granny Yarrow didn't look in the least bit scary. Her dress was pale blue and accented by a wide collar finished in her fine lace.

Willie said to the panel of amazed judges, "My granny."

Granny Yarrow nodded at the men. I couldn't help but notice that she was shaking.

Nannie was on her feet by then. She hurried to Granny Yarrow and took her from Willie, leading her to sit beside Star.

Star stopped blubbering and placed her hand on Granny Yarrow's knee.

Act II, Scene II.

"I'm not a bad boy," Willie started. "I've done some things I'm not real proud of." He stopped and looked up as if he were trying to read a list in his brain. "I've whipped a couple of boys. I've stole some sides of bacon. I've took a few apples and turnips and such. I shot out a school window to scare away that old teacher, Mr. Martin, but no one seemed to mind because they didn't like him no way."

Someone laughed and drew quick stares from the little panel of judges.

Willie looked toward Granny Yarrow. "My granny tried to raise me good. Guess I got just a little too much salt in me. Anyways, I've never been a choirboy, that's the truth. I talk

153

too much. I sip from the fruit jar too much. I like dancing and pretty girls." He glanced at Star and quickly looked back at the floor. "Still, being all those things and doing all I've done, I've never even thought about burning down a building. Anyways, why would I want to burn that old place?"

"That's what we were hoping you'd tell us," Mayor Brown said.

"I don't know what you're talking about," Willie mumbled.

"Lots of folks have seen you around the shoe factory," Mr. Roth piped.

"I live near there," Willie said.

The mayor said, "Some people feel it's you and your granny trying to keep people out of that swamp."

Willie didn't say anything.

"Why didn't you want people out there?" Mayor Brown asked.

It was Granny Yarrow who answered, "That property I've been livin' on all these years don't belong to me."

"Who does it belong to?" Mayor Brown asked.

"Miss Rhetta Harper," Granny Yarrow answered sadly.

Mayor Brown sighed. "And you were afraid you'd have to leave?"

Granny Yarrow shook her head in despair. "It's the only place I have to go. Willie's all that's left of my family. I don't bother no one. I just live my own little life . . ."

Nannie put her arm around Granny Yarrow and tried to comfort her.

Granny Yarrow said, "Willie was home the night of the burnin'. We had us a little talk. I fixed him some supper. We went to sleep."

The play seemed to be over. The only two suspects had been cleared. Now the real criminal had to be found. It would not be a Sunday picnic.

Nannie cleared her throat. "Harvey, we have our ways around here. We let these young men come forward and speak for themselves. Anyone able to come out and defend himself or admit his mistakes is welcome here. We don't hold much store in cowards." She glanced around the room.

A few people said, "That's right."

"You're saying to give the criminal a chance to come forward?" Mayor Brown asked.

Nannie said, "Yes."

Mayor Brown said, "How will this 'criminal' know what we're doing?"

"Because he's waiting with us here in this room."

16

The crowd waited for the criminal to confess his crime in much the same way a family waits for a groom who is late to his wedding. There is disgust that he would be so inconsiderate as to take up everyone's time without explanation. There is also a thirst for everything to be all right again. Relief. A deep breath. Things as they were.

Nannie sat on the bench beside Star with her feet crossed at the ankles. If she was impatient, her expression didn't show it. She seemed all-knowing. A true judge.

I knew what it was like to be at the receiving end of Nannie's judgment. To know that she knew what I had done even before I confessed. It was sheer pain. Star knew that pain, too. As did Mama and Cora and Aunt Nola and the boarders, as did anyone Nannie had authority over. And now some stranger was stewing and wondering which would be worse, confession and punishment or exposure and punishment. Love later, of course, but first punishment. How would the people punish a firebug? A torchbearer? A dream crusher?

Mr. Weeks stood up and stretched his legs. Mayor Brown started to do the same thing, but quickly Mr. Weeks slipped a hand on his shoulder and eased him back into his chair. With a crisp voice, Mr. Weeks said, "I burned the factory."

He must have been tired of waiting for the criminal to confess. Truth of it was I had almost admitted to the crime so we could all go home and sit on the porch and have lemonade.

Mr. Weeks wiped tears from his face. "I didn't know what

else to do." No, he was really confessing. He was crying. His wife was going to him. Lester was also walking to the front of the room with Betty and Rah-Rah behind him.

"I didn't mean to deceive you," Mr. Weeks continued. "I did have the money for the factory when we started, but you know how uneasy things are in the business world. My sources dried up. I sold everything I had, trying to come up with the cash; but it wasn't enough. I didn't want to disappoint all of you. You have been kind to my family and me. I thought if I delayed the building a bit, maybe I could find something else for the community. Another business, one not so expensive to start up. I hated to be the one to come in and cause all this commotion and then leave you with bad feelings."

What followed was the silence between sinners at a church testimony meeting. Then Mayor Brown spoke in a firm voice, saying, "A couple of you men see that Mr. Weeks makes it to the sheriff's office at Buck's Point."

The Weekses left slowly, all of them looking at the floor and excusing themselves through the crowd with muffled voices. Only Lester looked up for a moment. He glanced at Star. She was looking at him with a smile of sympathy on her face. He whispered to her, "It's all right. I know you did what you had to do."

As we stood up to leave, Star asked, "What will happen to Mr. Weeks?"

Before anyone answered her I said, "Lester told you his dad burned the factory the day after the fire, didn't he?"

Star nodded that he had.

"And you told Nannie when she came after you?" I asked.

"When it came down to accusing Wendall and Willie, I had to do something about it," Star said. "But I feel I've betrayed Lester."

"Don't be a goose," Mama said to Star. "You didn't do

anything wrong. You told the truth. That's important. It will work out for the best."

By the time we got to the front porch the Weekses were in Mr. Roth's automobile headed for Buck's Point.

"I expect some of us women should go over and bring Mrs. Weeks and the children back to the river house," Nannie said to the crowd.

"You mean they can stay?" Star asked, surprised.

"It's not their fault their daddy did what he did," Nannie started. "I expect it's all our faults because apparently none of us were close enough to Wally and his missus for them to come forward with their troubles."

No one challenged Nannie's judgment but, instead, talked among themselves as they went home.

We had sandwiches for supper, served plain except for a plate of relishes. No one seemed to mind the scant meal. Later in the evening Nannie made a peach cobbler and coffee.

Mr. Houser arrived in time to share the dessert with us. I didn't know he was coming and was embarrassed to have to meet him in my dungarees with my hair pulled back.

"You look quite all right, young lady," he assured me as Mama brought us together on the front porch.

He sat down knee to knee with Mama and pulled out some papers.

Mama looked over what he handed her.

"We're starting a barn-dance radio show," Mr. Houser said pleasantly. "Laurie would sing back-up there. I can arrange a place for the two of you to stay. You'll have the opportunity to work for the station, too, if you want, Mrs. Hargrove."

Mama said softly, "You're not offering Laurie much money."

My face flushed scarlet. I couldn't imagine why money had anything to do with it. I was being asked to sing on the radio. There would be money — someday. Plenty of money.

"It's about all I can give you, starting out," Mr. Houser said regretfully.

Mama didn't speak.

Mr. Houser said, "Let me leave the paperwork here with you until Friday. I'll come back then and we'll talk."

Mama nodded.

Mr. Houser stood up, patted me on the head, and went to his automobile.

When he was gone I turned to Mama. "What do you mean challenging him over the money? You're the one who cooked up this deal, and now you're dragging your feet —"

Mama pointed a finger at my face and said, "Don't you ever talk to me in that tone of voice again!"

"Yes, ma'am," I said, feeling my eyes fill with tears. "It just doesn't seem fair to offer me something as wonderful as singing on the radio and then risk losing the opportunity."

"It'll be fair," Mama said in a no-nonsense voice.

At breakfast the next day Mama stayed at the table after everyone had gone on to their day's business. Only Nannie was left in the kitchen, washing dishes.

"Laurie, sit down and talk with me," Mama said when I brought in the eggs I had gathered for Nannie.

Nannie glanced at us, and I caught the look in her eyes that said she knew what Mama was going to talk with me about. "You want me to leave, Sarah?" she asked.

"No, I'd rather you stayed," Mama said.

Nannie continued to wash the dishes.

"Laurie, I had to make a hard decision," Mama started.

"What decision?" I asked. My voice was sharper than I had planned.

"A decision about us. A decision about your singing career," Mama said firmly.

159

"I'm not going to have a singing career, am I?" I could feel a lump in my throat the size of a watermelon.

Mama reached out to touch my hand. "Yes, you are, but not —"

"But not right away," I added.

"It's the money —"

"Mama, you have plenty of money left over from selling the Packard. You told me it was enough to get me started," I begged.

"I'm using the money to rebuild the factory," Mama said.

Nannie wiped her hands on a towel and sat down beside Mama.

"That factory is more important than me?" I asked. "I can't believe you're putting other people before me. You've always hated the fact that Nannie has put other people before family, and here you are doing the same thing —"

"That's enough, Laurie," Nannie said.

"I imagine it is!" I jumped up and shoved my chair against the table.

"Listen to me, Laurie," Mama pleaded. "Sometimes a person has to do something because it's the right thing to do, not necessarily because it's the most pleasant thing to do."

"You mean something like opening a boardinghouse to support your family," I said.

Nannie turned toward me and said, "Laurie, your mama is having a hard enough time as it is —"

"No, Nan, she's right. It's exactly the same thing. I just never knew what a sacrifice was until now," Mama said.

Then Mama and Nannie hugged each other and cried on each other's shoulders. It was ridiculous. I was the one who was suffering, and they were weeping with joy. I sprinted up the stairs and locked myself in the attic. I planned to stay up there until the bloodsucking bats found me. They would leave only my bones for Mama and Nannie to dispose of. I lay on the dusty, old mattress and stared at the spider webs on the ceiling. It was at least a hundred degrees up there, and I began to suspect that the heat would kill me before the bats flew out of the chimney.

Someone tapped at the door.

"Go away. I'm dying," I whimpered.

"It's me," Star said. "Let me in."

"Go away."

"Let me in," she insisted.

I got up and opened the door. "Come in. You can watch me die."

Star said, "Good grief."

"Mama won't let me go to Atlanta. She's using the money for the factory."

"I heard."

"I'm stuck here," I cried. "Stuck here in Guthrie like —"

Star finished with, "Like me."

The great difference in being able to choose whether to leave and in *having* to stay hit me something like the cold water at the end of a long dive. It took my breath away and shot me back to reality whether I wanted to face it or not.

"I'm sorry," was all I could say.

Star sat down beside me and let me cry on her shoulder. "It'll work out," she assured me.

"I think I hate Mama and Nannie. It's taken them all their lives to grow up, and they want me to grow up in an afternoon."

Star patted my back. "I expect a lot of growing up takes place in only an afternoon."

I sat up. "What do you mean?"

"I mean growing up when your husband doesn't come back from the lumber mill," Star said.

161

"Or when your husband doesn't come back from war," I added.

Star got up and looked out the window, across the valley to that wide world she so wanted to touch.

I walked over beside her and said, "Life's what you make it."

"Let's go somewhere cooler," she said, smiling.

So we went downstairs.

The Old Widder's Club met Thursday like clockwork. They shut the door to the parlor while they talked, and they talked for about three hours, not even breaking to refill the lemonade pitcher.

Even the boarders lost interest in their doings and retired to sun away the afternoon on the front porch. Finally, Nannie scooted everyone home and called Mama, Star, and me into the kitchen.

Star poured lemonade for everyone and said, "Nan, you ladies sure must have had plenty of gossip to share this afternoon."

Nannie took a drink of her lemonade. "We didn't gossip. We discussed."

"What did you discuss?" I asked.

Mama sat quietly.

Nannie said, "We discussed letting bygones be bygones." She glanced at Mama and smiled.

"What does she mean?" Star asked.

"It means the Old Widder's Club is going to invest in Guthrie like Sarah has done," Nannie said. "It means that if Sarah needs her money for other things, like starting a singing career for someone we all love, then she can use it for that."

I got up and threw my arms around Nannie's neck. "You don't have to do that. I'm willing to wait."

"I don't *have* to do it, I *want* to do it. This is something I have control over, and I want to make the right choice. Nola and Rhetta and Fannie all have choices like that to make. Mr. Roosevelt is promising a New Deal on the radio. I'm offering a new deal here."

"What will happen to Mr. Weeks?" Star asked.

"Well, the last time Mr. Avartoz returned from Kansas City he told us how that community is growing and that they desperately need lumber. I think that might be something for us to check into. The people of Guthrie do know how to make boards. Hundreds of miles of them," Nannie stated. "I think Mayor Brown and the others would let Mr. Weeks off with two years of hard labor getting our new lumber mill running."

I felt like applauding. It was a story with a happy ending. And there would still be a factory, not as fanciful as shoes but more familiar. I knew it would mean changes in Guthrie, but I began to suspect that all changes weren't bad.

Later that evening, after everyone had gone to bed, I slipped downstairs to go to the outhouse. When I returned I found Nannie sitting at the kitchen table holding a pen above a piece of stationery.

"What are you doing up, Laurie?" she asked.

"I was outside," I said.

Nannie took off her spectacles and laid them on the table. "I can't see so good by artificial light."

"Do you need some help?" I asked.

"Yes," she said as she scooted a chair aside for me.

I sat down, turned the empty sheet of paper toward me, and took the pen from Nannie's outstretched hand. "What do you want me to write?" I asked.

Nannie breathed deeply and said, "Dear Eli."

• • •

In honor of the new lumber deal and my singing career and the Old Widder's Club's changed attitudes, Nannie fixed a wingding of a meal the next Sunday. She served both ham and veal, with at least one dish of each of the vegetables from the garden, three kinds of bread, and a half dozen different types of pie. We were also having ice cream, and Mr. Avartoz was in charge of its creation.

Besides Aunt Nola's family, Nannie invited Lester, Wendall, and Nathan.

Before lunch, Star sat on the porch swing and looked into Lester's eyes. Cora and Wendall sat arm in arm on the steps and whispered to each other. Nathan and I looked across the yard.

Nathan seemed to be a million miles away. Finally, he turned toward me and said in almost a whisper, "I hear that Houser fellow gave you a contract."

"That's right. Mama and I are leaving for Atlanta this fall," I said.

Nathan turned away.

I reached over and touched his arm. I felt a slight tremble there as if the living had touched the dead. And I knew what was dead — our feelings for each other.

"It was nice of Nan to invite me here today. Nice of her to invite Lester," Nathan said.

"But Lester makes you think about Betty, right?" I asked.

Nathan nodded that it did.

"I'm sure Betty needs you to comfort her right now. The whole factory incident was embarrassing," I heard myself say with a hollow voice.

Nathan shuffled. "Betty is alone," he said, mostly to himself.

"Go to her," I said.

"No hard feelings?" Nathan asked.

I kissed him on the cheek. "No hard feelings."

The tears I held back made my brain float. I barely heard Nannie call us to the table. I found my seat with the help of Star and Cora.

Nannie prayed over the meal, and even Mr. Avartoz bowed his head. The table seemed crowded, so, with little fanfare, Nannie stood up and swept the plate set for Jesus from the table. "Seems to me the Bible says that when Jesus comes back, he won't have much time to sit down for a meal," Nannie said softly. She then looked long at Eli's plate before she also slipped it off the table.

We feasted for about an hour and then retired to the parlor to sing around the piano. Aunt Nola cranked out a few old hymns, then Mama played some new tunes we had learned in New York. We all sang at the top of our lungs.

We were a great choir, blending together as only a family can, with no voice any greater than the others, and all voices finding strength in those around them.

Mama played "Down in the Valley," and we all sang our parts. We had plenty of sopranos and altos, and even Lester managed a baritone of sorts. But on the last verse of the song a fine, deep bass joined in.

We turned toward the parlor door. There, bigger than life, stood Uncle Eli. With a tear-choked voice he asked, "What's for supper, Nan?"

There had never before been music as sweet as the words between Nannie and Mama and Star and Uncle Eli that followed. Sweet, healing words. Words sung together with the hidden melody of love and the perfect harmony of family.

The one road to Guthrie was to be extended beyond the dam on the Wigerstat in order to connect the new lumber mill with the main highway. By the time Mama and I were to leave for

Atlanta that autumn the rocks had been graded away with a piece of equipment the Old Widder's Club had purchased for the town. Wendall drove the truck that pulled the grader, and he was saving his salary to build a little house for Cora and himself.

Nathan and Lester had invented a new saw that was guaranteed to double the production of the old mill. They had been working hard at the factory site, with Betty and Star brightening their days with lunch baskets and lemonade.

I waved at them as Mama drove the truck up the main road. I felt tears fill my eyes and an emptiness in my heart for all the things that had been and were going to continue to be without me.

Mama said as comfort, "If you take enough steps forward you'll end up back home."

I smiled and reached for my guitar. Those seemed like just the right words for a hillbilly song.